ANISHA

ACCIDENTAL DETECTIVE

kiDNapPeD!

D0780736

SERENA PATEL

Illustrated by Emma McCann

USBORNE

CHAPTER 1

DISASTER!

"**NO, NO, NO,** this is terrible! I said **pink** carnations. If I wanted **red** ones, I would have asked for **RED** ones!" yells my Aunty Bindi.

She's making a right racket. Her fists are clenched and her face is turning a funny purply colour – I'm a bit worried that her head might actually erupt in a big purple slime explosion as she screams at the flower delivery man. This is already the third time she's sent the poor man back and he looks like he's going to cry.

I slump in the chair and bury my head in my book, **Life, the Universe and Everything**, to try to shut out the noise. I just wish I could get some peace and quiet around here. Dad says I should be reading "more appropriate books for girls my age". I'm not sure what kind of books those are, but I like reading about time, space and numbers. Numbers are great, they make sense – unlike people. You'd think this too if you lived with my family.

The delivery man apologizes like his life depends on it. "**I'm so sorry, madam.** I just deliver the flowers, as I explained before. Perhaps you should ring the shop and tell them exactly what you want."

"**I DID** tell them. **It's not rocket science,** is it? I want my flowers and I want them pink. Is that too much to ask?" And with that, she **slams** the front door so hard that it bounces back and hits her in the face.

"Aunty, this is just a suggestion, but maybe you should calm down. Getting stressed isn't good for your health," I say, as I watch her rubbing her nose. Mum says these kinds of helpful things to my dad all the time. He gets stressed out too – not by flowers but by his job as a lawyer for **BUNDI, BANDU AND BHASKAR LLP**. I'm not sure exactly what he does, but it seems to involve going all red in the face and shouting down the phone a lot. When I grow up, I'm going to work in a lab where it's clean and quiet and I don't have to see a lot of people. That would be my number-one dream job.

"This wedding is going to be a disaster, a first-class disaster!" Aunty Bindi wails. She's been speaking all high-pitched like this ever since she started planning her wedding. **THE WEDDING OF THE YEAR!** The wedding that is happening **TOMORROW**. She's marrying her "sweetie pie". (That's what she calls him – **URGH!**) His real name is Tarnvir, except only his mum calls him that.

Everyone else calls him by his nickname, Tony.

According to the grown-ups, a wedding is a really big deal: flowers, frilly dresses and a ridiculously large cake with little people on top and expensive crystals round the edges. It all seems totally unnecessary to me. For their honeymoon they're going to this resort in Spain which has the world's biggest theme park – is it me or is that a **WEIRD** place to go on your honeymoon? Uncle Tony loves it though – theme parks are his favourite thing, as well as music by an old rock-and-roll star I'd never heard of, **ELVIS PRESLEY.** And his favourite person in the whole wide world is, of course, my Aunty Bindi. She loves what he loves – they are so **CRINGE** when they're together.

But the worst thing about this wedding is that Aunty Bindi decided I should be a bridesmaid and I have to wear the most awful lengha, which is made up of a bright orange embroidered top with an itchy gold frill on the sleeves and neckline and a floor-length skirt in the same colour.

Now, I love Aunty Bindi. Out of my whole ridiculously big family she is my favourite aunt and she does make me laugh. She used to look after me a lot when I was little cos she lived with us. And even though she can be a bit much sometimes we've always been **SO** close, even though we're **SO** different. Aunty Bindi is really kind hearted and she would do anything for anyone, especially me. I would do mostly anything for her but when it comes to itchy bridesmaid lenghas, I'd really rather wear a lab coat. Mum said I'd better not suggest that to my aunty though, especially with how crazy all this wedding stuff is making her.

"You know what, I'll ring Tony. He'll calm me down. He always knows what to say," she witters, as she taps on her phone with her sparkly false nails. Aunty Bindi loves things that **sparkle**. She has sparkly bags, sparkly clothes – she's even been talking about getting a sparkly pink car. I've told her

I will not be getting in it with her.

I take a **deep breath** and try to get back into my book, but the quiet doesn't last very long.

"**HUMPFH!** He's not even answering. What else could he possibly have to do that's more important than speaking to **ME**?" she whines, running her sparkly nails through her big hair.

I'm not sure what the right answer is to that question so I keep my mouth firmly shut. Aunty Bindi is not usually this whiney. She can be **squawky**, for sure, but this is next-level annoying! She has barely stopped for breath. "Do you realize the wedding is tomorrow? I'm having my **mehndi***" (see footnote) "done at lunchtime today and I've got a huge zit on my nose and now probably a big bruise

---

* The first time I saw mehndi, I think I was about four or five years old and I thought it was a tube of Mum's fancy hand cream. I squeezed a load onto my hands and was a bit puzzled when they turned a greeny-black colour. So, not wanting to get in trouble for having mucky hands, I wiped them on Mum and Dad's new white cotton bedspread. Mum later explained that mehndi is basically a dye that is used to colour hair or decorate the hands and feet with swirly patterns on special occasions. How was I supposed to know? The writing on the label was in Hindi!

as well, all the relatives are arriving any minute, and the florist can't even get the garlands right!"

She pauses dramatically for effect and flops onto our green corduroy sofa with the back of her hand to her head like she's about to faint. Aunty Bindi really likes to be dramatic. I firmly believe that she sometimes thinks she's in a Bollywood movie. This one time she got really upset because she and Uncle Tony had had an argument, so she sat by the window sobbing and singing **"TERE BINA ZINDAGI"**, which is a really old Indian love song, at the top of her voice. She was so loud and out of tune that the

neighbours complained – well, mostly Mr Bogof from **number 62**, he's always complaining about something. I had to admit though, on this occasion, the singing was pretty bad. I put my headphones on with earmuffs over the top and I could still hear her! Having relatives living with you can be hard work.

Right now, I really want to ask Aunty Bindi how the big zit on her nose affects her having her mehndi done on her hands and feet. But maybe it's not the right time for questions. Then I think, maybe she's starting a new trend? **NOSE MEHNDI!** You know, nose mehndi could really take off. In fact, what's she complaining about? It could actually cover up the **planet-sized spot** that is emerging on her nose. (It looks a little like **Saturn**, or maybe **Mars**, and it's getting redder by the minute.)

Mehndi is a bit swirly twirly for me. I prefer right angles, but I'm guessing that mehndi squares might look a bit odd. I'm sure it will look nice on

Aunty Bindi though, as she's a swirly twirly kind of person. Actually, if Aunty Bindi does have mehndi on her nose, it might draw attention away from my horrid orange-and-gold lengha.

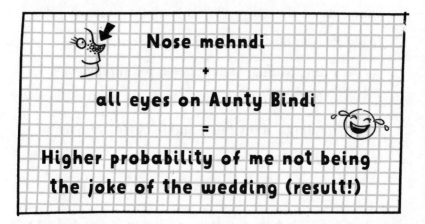

Nose mehndi

+

all eyes on Aunty Bindi

=

Higher probability of me not being the joke of the wedding (result!)

I think about telling Aunty Bindi about my analysis of the situation, but instead I say, "I'm sure it will all work out in the end." This is something else my mum says a lot, mostly when everything is going wrong. Mum likes to see the positive in every situation. She says when she was growing up everyone was much more **chilled out**. It all sounds very inefficient. I like things to be organized and neat – it's kind of my thing. My family are so **messy** and **noisy** that sometimes I think I must have been adopted or beamed down by aliens.

Just then my earlier wish is granted and Mum comes down the stairs. "What is all the noise about? Is everything okay, Bindi?" she calls out.

"It's fine, Mum," I shout back, rolling my eyes.

"It is **NOT** fine! It's all a disaster, **Didi**!*"
Aunty Bindi grabs my mum and starts to cry noisily into her shoulder.

Why do Indian weddings have to take so long

✿★✩★✭✿★✿✩✿★✿✿✿★✿✿✿★✿✿✿★✿✿★✿✿✩★✿✿✭★✿✩✿★✿✩✿

* Aunty Bindi calls my mum Didi, which is weird because her name is actually Bhavana, but they tell me Didi is the Hindi word for sister. My Hindi is not great. I only know the bad words that Granny taught me. In our house Mum and Dad speak mainly English and so do most of my relatives, apart from a few Gujarati or Punjabi words thrown in, depending on which side of the family they are on. Granny speaks mainly Hindi because she was brought up in Mumbai in India and when she was growing up she loved all the old Bollywood movies. Dad can speak Hindi, Gujarati and Punjabi, but pretends he can't understand especially when Granny is telling him off. Mum calls it selective hearing. Anyway, some of our family call Granny by a different word – Ba – which is Gujarati for Granny. But I've always just called her Granny.

– they don't just last one day, they go on for a whole week! Yesterday there was a ceremony in the house with a priest and lots of singing. Mum had to paint Aunty Bindi with turmeric on her face and arms and legs – she looked like a big yellow monster. Granny said it's supposed to be a special blessing and also it's good for your skin. Well, they're never doing that to me – not that I'm ever getting married!

Today is the mehndi party so the marquee will be filled with family again. Not just a few relatives either – Mum said we're expecting a hundred guests! I didn't know that we were related to that many people, but Mum said her and Aunty Bindi's side of the family is really big! I look through the patio doors at the end of our living room into the marquee and out to the garden beyond. Right at the bottom behind the hedge is Granny's greenhouse. No matter how packed the house and marquee get, no one will go near it. No one is ever, ever allowed to enter the greenhouse.

"There there, we can't have the bride crying, can we?" Mum says, stroking Bindi's hair while pushing a tissue towards her. She's good at this making-it-better thing. I guess she's had a lot of practice growing up with Aunty Bindi as her little sister. I can't imagine having a little brother or sister. It might have been nice to have someone to share theories and do experiments with, but the probability they would be like me is quite low. Not many people are.

I shuffle in the armchair and slide down as far as I can without falling onto the floor. I am **NOT** good at this emotional stuff. It makes me feel all itchy and uncomfortable, **PLUS** no one listens to what I think anyway. Grown-ups like to ruffle your hair and comment on how much you've grown, but they don't really care what you think about important stuff. They just want you to stay quiet and behave – when, actually, I wish **THEY** would just **STAY QUIET** and **BEHAVE**.

Just then the house phone rings on the sideboard behind me. I jump up out of my comfy chair to answer it, glad to have a distraction from Aunty Bindi's sobbing.

"Hello?" I say quickly.

"Who is that?" asks a gruff, heavily-accented voice. I recognize it straight away – its Uncle Tony's brother Vikram (everyone calls him Ricky for short).

"It's me," I answer.

"Who's me?" Uncle Ricky asks.

"Uncle Ricky, it's Anisha!" I say, getting annoyed.

"Ah, Anni, it's me, Uncle Ricky. Can I speak to your mum?" he says.

"Hang on." I sigh and hold the phone out for Mum to take. I **hate** being called Anni, though the grown-ups in my family seem to think it's cute!

YUCK!

Mum reaches for the phone with her free hand while Bindi remains attached to her other arm.

"Yes, hello? Oh, Ricky, how are you? Okay, well that sounds…interesting, but I'm not sure it's appropriate. Well, I don't think…but, don't you think…okay, alright, I'll speak to you later."

And with that she hangs up the phone, still frowning from her conversation.

"What did Uncle Ricky want?" I ask suspiciously. Uncle Ricky never calls unless he wants something. I think Uncle Tony gets a bit fed up with him sometimes. But why would he call Mum?

"Nothing to worry about. Just boring wedding stuff." Mum smiles brightly – a little too brightly – not answering my question at all.

Bindi doesn't notice any of this and continues sniffling into Mum's shoulder. I have to get out of here, even if it's just for a bit. I jump up and say, "I'm just going to Milo's."

Mum waves with her free hand and says, "Don't be long, Anni. Remember the mehndi party is starting in a little while, people will be arriving soon."

"Yes, Mum," I answer, even though I can't think of anything worse than a house full of people **AND** having to talk to them for hours about swirly-twirly mehndi.

I grab my backpack and head for the front door. When I enter the hallway I notice an envelope sticking halfway through the letter box. Did the postman come already? Mum's always moaning that he's late; she'll be pleased he's been early for once.

I bend down and grab the envelope. There's no stamp on it and on the front someone's scrawled **To the Bride**. I turn the envelope over and the flap slides open, revealing part of the letter inside. One word jumps out at me:

KIDNAPPED

My hands are shaking now. I quickly open the front door and look around. The street outside is empty. I shut the door and look at the half-opened envelope. What do I do? Without really thinking, I pull the note out to read it. The paper is thick and looks expensive. Don't ask me why, but I smell it. It has a sharp odour – it's really familiar but I can't think what it is.

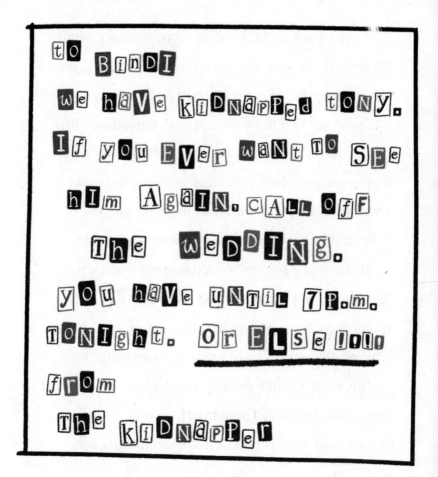

TO BINDI

WE HAVE KIDNAPPED TONY.

IF YOU EVER WANT TO SEE

HIM AGAIN, CALL OFF

THE WEDDING.

YOU HAVE UNTIL 7P.M.

TONIGHT. OR ELSE !!!!

FROM

THE KIDNAPPER

I read it again to make sure I haven't
misunderstood. Someone has kidnapped Uncle Tony
on the day before the wedding? Is this a **joke**? Who
would joke about something like that?

I peek back into the living room at Aunty Bindi, who is still blowing her nose (how much snot does she have in there?), and Mum, who is still trying to reassure her that the wedding isn't cursed and that her zit doesn't look that bad. I realize that if I go in there now and show them this note, it will be like a **volcano** erupting. So I decide, there and then, to keep it to myself until I can make sense of it.

It could just be a joke – although it's really not that funny. But it sounds real. **KIDNAP?!** A shiver runs down my spine. I'm not sure what to do. Why would anyone want to kidnap Uncle Tony?

But wait! There's usually a logical reason for most things that happen. There **must** be a logical explanation for this note. I just need to work out what it is.

I need my best friend. Milo will know what to do. And that's how I end up running like lightning down the road to **number 58**.

CHAPTER 2

ANIMAL BOY

Milo Moon is my best friend and the only person –
outside of my family – that I trust with my life. The
main thing you need to know about Milo is that he
is the kindest person ever.

He **really** loves animals. He loves them a **LOT**.
This will sound weird, but he thinks he can talk to
them like Doctor Dolittle does. He says he has A.I.
(Animal Intuition). I've never seen any evidence to
support this theory, but Milo has been really, really
sure he has it ever since he saw a programme about
people who think they have it. He also has bright
orange hair, freckles on his nose, a bit of a wonky
smile and, like me, he doesn't really fit in with the

cool crowd at school – that's how we ended up being best friends.

I can hear noise (as usual) as I run up the front path to Milo's house.

"**GET IT OUT! GET RID OF IT RIGHT NOW!**" It's the voice of Mrs Moon, Milo's mum, coming through the open living-room window.

Milo comes shooting out of the red front door and almost knocks me over. He's struggling to hold on to Yasmine, his very round ginger tabby cat, but she's squirming and hissing and looking like she's not happy **AT ALL**.

"Yasmine brought home a mouse again," Milo explains over the head of the cranky cat.

"Well, that's nothing new," I say, shrugging. "She's always doing that."

"She put it in my mum's bed," he continues.

"Ah," I say.

"Yep, Mum is not happy," says Milo. "She's

24

threatening to take Yasmine to a shelter, but I can't let that happen. She's my best friend – apart from you, of course. I know people don't believe I actually have **Animal Intuition**, but me and Yas had a really good talk last night and she agreed with me: it's hard being ginger – people just don't get us. We might look different, and yes, our hair is orange, but we still have feelings, you know? Cats are very sensitive, loving creatures."

He cuddles Yasmine close to his face. She squirms and hisses but Milo barely seems to notice.

Time is already zooming past – I **have** to tell Milo about the **KIDNAP** note (although I'm still not convinced it can be real...yet). "Milo, I know you're worried about Yas, but I need to tell you something **URGENT**! No one else knows about this and it might be nothing, but you can't tell anyone, promise?"

"What is it? I'm not sure I want to promise anything until I know. You could be about to tell me you're an **international jewel thief** and that would make me an accessory!" Milo frowns at me.

"Just promise, Milo. I'm not an international jewel thief. Be logical! I think you'd know by now if I was," I snap.

"Oh, okay," he says, sounding a bit disappointed. "I promise I won't say anything."

I check no one's around and then drop my voice to a whisper anyway, just in case. "This will sound like complete nonsense, but I have reason to believe that **someone has kidnapped Uncle Tony** and they're demanding that the wedding is called off."

"**WHAT?!**"

Milo shouts.

"**Shhhh!** It's top-secret and it might not even be real. I mean, c'mon, this is Birmingham not the Bronx – nothing ever happens round here. Aunty Bindi can't know until we're sure what's going on. She's already in **meltdown mode**. If I tell her this she will explode."

"She's already a bit of a firecracker," says Milo. "So, what are you going to **DO**, Neesh?"

"Me?"

Why did I have to be the one to find the note? I think to myself. Doesn't anyone understand: **I DON'T LIKE DRAMA!** If I go back and show the note to my family, they'll start panicking and squawking at each other like a bunch of birds, making things worse. It'll be a complete disaster then. Bindi will be a **TOTAL** nightmare – even more than usual!

Milo carries on at me: "Yes, you. Look, I know you like a quiet life, but this is **YOUR** auntie's wedding. You can't just sit back and do nothing."

"I wasn't thinking of doing nothing, just nothing **overt**," I say.

"Over what?" Milo says, confused.

"Overt – it means obvious. What I mean is, we should take a step back. Examine the facts. It could just be a joke after all. A good scientist always does their research before anything else. We have to identify who sent the note before Aunty Bindi finds out and **TOTALLY FREAKS**! The wedding is tomorrow so we don't have much time. We need to examine the note for clues and make a list of people who might want to ruin the wedding."

Observing suspicious behaviour
+
examining evidence
+
preparing for action
=
Staying out of trouble
+
avoiding drama

"But then what?" asks Milo. "What if we find out your uncle really has been kidnapped and who did it, but they won't give him back? We're just kids, if you hadn't noticed, Neesh – we can't go telling big, bad kidnappers what to do."

"Well...I haven't thought that far ahead, have I? We'll deal with that if we come to it. Scientists know there are always several possible outcomes and they should be prepared for any eventuality." I nod as though I know what I'm talking about. "Come on, Milo, we need to get to work! **We have evidence to examine!**"

"Ooh, like detectives! Don't you have a magnifying glass at home? We used it for our biology project last term, remember?" Milo glances down at Yasmine the cat, who's now purring in his arms. "We'll talk later," he tells her sternly. "I think you should go and think about what you've done." Yasmine **meows** at him, leaps down and lands neatly on her paws. She darts away round the back of Milo's house, probably to catch more mice.

"Mum! I'm just going up the road with Neesh!" Milo shouts into the house and pulls the front door closed with a click before his mum can reply.

Milo and I have lived exactly six doors away from each other on Jewel Street ever since I can

remember. As I said, I'd trust him with my life...
except when he's not really **paying attention**.
Unfortunately, this happens quite a lot, especially if
there is an animal nearby.

As we walk back up the road, Milo chattering
about Yasmine the cat, I think about the note and
silently praise myself for staying calm. Any sort
of upset usually brings me out in a rash, but today
I am in control and I'm going to figure it all out
without any fuss.

There's more to this than just a random kidnap;
I have a feeling. We can solve this and save my
family loads of unnecessary stress. I feel quite proud
of myself for a second...until I see a black beast of
a car pulling up by my house. I suddenly feel very
cold, even though the **sun** has come out. My feet
drag and I slow down to a snail's pace.

"Why are you walking so slowly all of a sudden?
Aren't we in a hurry?" Milo asks.

"**Shhh, it's them!**" I whisper loudly, and grab Milo's arm to slow him down even more.

"Who's **them**?" Milo asks, trying to pull himself free of my grasp. "And can you let go of my jumper? Mum only bought it for me last week and she'll get cross if it's all stretched."

I let go of his sleeve but keep my hand on his arm. "My soon-to-be cousins," I say with another shudder. "**THE EVIL TWINS!**"

Milo starts giggling. He has never met the evil twins or he wouldn't be laughing right now. The evil

twins are Mindy and Manny, Uncle Tony's kids from his first marriage, and the meanest kids I know. If you're wondering how mean a couple of ten-year-olds can be, let me tell you: **MEAN.**

The first time they came to our house last Christmas, Mum said I should be nice and make them feel welcome. I didn't know what they were like back then, so while the grown-ups were doing their chitting-chatting (that's what Granny Jas calls it) over cups of tea and samosas, I invited the twins up to my room. **BIG MISTAKE!**

I was showing them the chapter in my book on tensile strength, friction and adhesion. The twins said we should test out the maximum weight that a roll of duct tape can hold up on my bedroom wall. I thought, **Ooh, science experiment, let's do it**.

So they did.

By sticking me to the wall and taping my mouth up so I couldn't shout for help.

It was **ages** before anyone found me. And when I tried to tell Mum the twins were evil, she just said it must be a misunderstanding and I shouldn't be melodramatic. Me? Melodramatic!

Evil twins
+
duct tape
+
force of gravity
=
Ouch, everywhere!

First to get out of the big black car is the chauffeur. Uncle Tony is quite rich because he owns a chain of well-known phone shops and that's how he met Aunty Bindi. She went into one of his shops looking for a new phone and, being totally clueless, needed some help. Uncle Tony was there checking on some new stock that had come in and he said it was love at first sight over the **Samisungs**, as he calls them. I hate when they talk all soppy.

Anyway, his chauffeur is called Mustaf and he's a giant – not an actual giant, of course, but he's very tall. He wears a long black coat and a black turban around his head. He has a thick bushy beard and the most impressive moustache I've ever seen. It actually curls up at the ends. I've never heard Mustaf speak but then I'm not sure I want to. In my head his voice is **deep and scary**.

Mustaf opens the passenger door and a bony hand reaches for the door handle as Manny steps out onto the pavement. His dark hair is set into concrete spikes, probably with half a tub of gel. He wears square-framed spectacles and is dressed all in black: jeans, T-shirt with a skull on it, black-and-grey shirt over the top and trainers – all dark and mean-looking like a vampire from that show Mindy's always watching. He's got his nose stuck to a tablet – probably on one of those skateboarding games he likes. He almost trips over the kerb as he steps out of the car.

His sister, Mindy, follows. She has sleek black hair barely parted in the middle so that it just about reveals her nose and mouth. I don't think I've ever seen her full face. She's wearing her usual black coat with the oversized buttons, and a black-and-purple scarf round her neck. In one hand she carries her precious notebook, one of those spiral-bound ones, which she takes everywhere. It's probably full of spells and hexes and curses. Under her other arm is her pet dog Bella. Bella is skinny with pointy ears and she's also completely bald except for some tufty bits of black fur on her ears and tail.

Bella's head turns in my direction, and for a terrifying moment our eyes meet. She **yelps**.

Mindy turns to see what Bella is barking at. There's no time to hide – she spots us. The hairs on my arms stand up and my mouth suddenly feels very dry. Mindy nudges Manny and nods in our direction.

"What do we do? Run? You said they're evil and now they're coming this way!" whispers Milo.

"Just stay calm," I say, even though my heart is pounding and my hands feel sweaty.

"Well, if it isn't our soon-to-be cousin-in-law, **Aniiiiiisha.**" Mindy draws out my name and then smirks.

Bella the dog stares at me like she knows something I don't.

"Hello, Mindy, hello, Manny, how are you both?" I try to steady my voice, wishing they'd just go away. Talking to people is not my favourite thing to do – especially when the people are **EVIL**!

"Oh, we're good, aren't we, Manny? **Really good!**" Mindy grins at us. This makes me even more on edge.

"Are we? Oh, yeah, I mean, yeah, really good!" Manny agrees like a nodding-dog toy.

"That's…erm…good then, I guess." I smile nervously.

"And who's this?"

Mindy flashes a sickly smile at Milo.

"This is Milo, my friend. Hadn't you better be getting inside? Aunty Bindi is **so excited** to see you," I reply.

"**URGH!**" Manny exclaims, but Mindy nudges him hard in the ribs. "Oh, I mean, **urgh urgh**,

I have a cough. I don't know where that came from—"

"Er, anyway," Mindy interrupts, "yes, we'd better be going inside. See you later, Anisha. Maybe you can show us some of your interesting science books again." Mindy backs away, still smiling. Bella the dog has fallen asleep in her other arm. Manny follows them, still making that weird **URGH** sound.

"What was all that about?" Milo mumbles as the twins skulk away. "I bet that dog was dreaming about quantum physics. I think she'd love that book you're reading. Anyway they didn't seem so bad. Why exactly do you think they're **evil**?"

I don't say anything about last Christmas to Milo. He always likes to see the best in people. Instead I say, "They're just not very nice people, Milo, trust me. They must be here for the mehndi party. The groom's family wouldn't normally come, but Aunty Bindi asked for them to be here – something about **bonding with her new stepchildren**."

"Hey, Neesh, if they're so mean, maybe they delivered the note to freak everyone out and cause a bit of trouble, like a joke or something."

"I wouldn't put it past them," I grumble. "But no, I know for a fact they've been at that fancy boarding school they go to. Bindi was telling Mum about it yesterday. She said that Mustaf was only going to be picking them up this morning, so they wouldn't have had a chance to put the note through our letter box. Anyway, they're bad but I don't think even they are **that** bad. Come on, let's go inside and begin our investigations."

But before we can do anything further, an ear-splitting scream from inside my house makes us both jump!

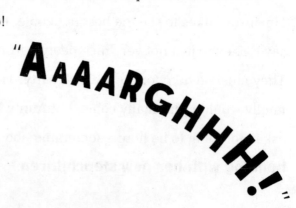

"**AAAARGHHH!**"

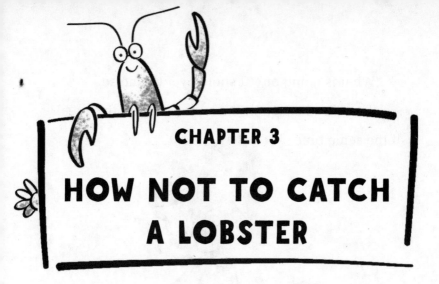

CHAPTER 3

HOW NOT TO CATCH A LOBSTER

Milo and I scramble up the steps into the house and stumble into the living room, looking for whoever – or whatever – could be making that awful noise. Aunty Suki, my mum's other sister, comes running towards us from the kitchen, waving a mop around and screeching at the top of her voice:

"**LOBSTERRRR!**"

Aunty Bindi shrieks and totters on her tiptoes – she's standing on the sofa in her pink spotty dressing gown. She's got big fat rollers in her hair and some kind of bright green goo face mask on. She's obviously getting ready for the nose mehndi later.

"What is going on?" I shout over the noise.

"There's a lobster on the loose!" they both squeal at the same time.

I notice Uncle Ricky has arrived and is lurking by the entrance to the marquee. "Granny Jas is making lobster curry later. I don't think the lobster likes that idea," he remarks, not looking up from his phone.

"No need to panic," says Mum in her sing-song-just-keep-calm voice as she comes downstairs. "It's probably more frightened of you than you are of it."

"I am **NOT** panicking," Dad huffs, dashing downstairs behind her. "Just someone, for goodness' sake, **GET IT**!" He grabs the mop from Suki and thrusts it towards me. "Here, Anni, you're strong. You can bash it with the mop!"

"I don't want it!" I say, pushing the mop back towards Dad. "And I am **NOT** bashing a lobster!"

"Let me get to it!" Milo pleads through the commotion. "I can talk it round."

"Oh, Bhagavan!* Just pass me the mop," orders Granny Jas. "Honestly, I have never known such a fuss. How do you think they are getting their food in the villages back home?"

* The word Granny uses the most in our house is "Bhagavan". She says it when things go wrong, when she can't get up out of the comfy armchair, when her knees are hurting and when Aunty Bindi is annoying everyone...which is quite often. If you don't know or haven't already guessed, it means "Oh God!"

If you ever meet my Granny Jas you'll see she is tiny but **FIERCE**. No one knows exactly how old she is. She has long grey hair always tied back in a plait and she wears a sari every day, pleated to perfection. She is the wrinkliest old person I know, but still as quick as a fox, and she leaps past me with her arm outstretched for the mop.

Milo blocks the door to the kitchen. "Maybe I should try to talk to the lobster. Your mum's right, he's probably more scared than all of you. You **ARE** trying to cook him, remember?"

Granny harrumphs but thankfully doesn't go into the kitchen to bash the lobster. I follow Milo as he slowly backs away in the direction of the intrepid invertebrate (I've been watching too much David Attenborough with him). He whispers to me, "**DID YOU KNOW** that lobsters have ten legs? Imagine if humans had ten legs! How fast could we get to school?"

"I think we should concentrate on how fast the lobster is getting away," I reply.

"Well, I read that some lobsters live to be one hundred – if they don't get cooked by your granny, that is! Maybe he deserves to get away," Milo remarks, pushing his hand against the kitchen door.

As Milo slowly walks through the doorway, I see it. The lobster is about as long as I am from my head to my waist. He's a dark browny-green colour with little specks of electric blue dotted along his back. And he's scuttling across the floor towards the back door, making a run for it, claws click-clacking as he goes. I just **KNOW** this is not going to go well.

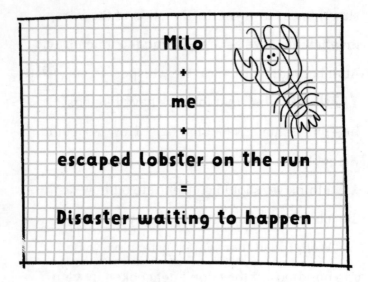

Milo

+

me

+

escaped lobster on the run

=

Disaster waiting to happen

"Careful now," Milo murmurs. "You have to approach from behind or he could get you with his claw. Also, I saw a documentary once that showed how lobsters wee out of their faces, so maybe stay back."

Milo inches round until he is behind the lobster, then lurches forward with his hands outstretched. Not seeing the mop bucket in front of him, he trips, landing face first. I make a leap to save Milo as he's falling, but the floor is slippery, my feet skid and my

legs flail as I lose
my balance and
hit the tiles with
a **THUD** –
which is just
as painful as
it sounds.

When I look
up, I see the evil
twins are standing
there, smirking
at me. Where did they come from?

"What are you looking at?" I say, annoyed.
"Never seen someone fall over before?"

"Not quite so spectacularly." Manny laughs,
holding his tummy.

"So irresponsible, letting a lobster wander around
like that. However did it escape? We could get Bella
to catch it if you need some help," suggests Mindy
menacingly.

"I think we can manage," I say, looking up at Mindy and her vampire dog. Bella's letting out a low **GROWL** and baring her pointy teeth, so we'd better do something fast. I'm not a fan of this lobster but even I don't want to see him end up as dog food!

"**Quick, grab him!**" I shout to Milo, rushing to my feet and making a final dive for the lobster before it disappears out the door – but just as I do, the lobster faces me. Everything slows down. I'm mid-air and he's looking straight at me over his enormous pincers. I could be imagining it, but I swear he just grinned at me! Then he does the most disgusting thing. Yes, you guessed it…

He does a wee 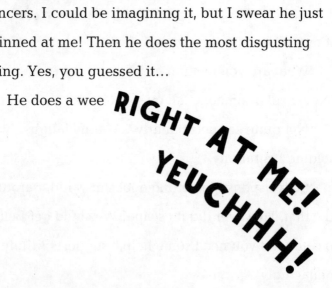 RIGHT AT ME! YEUCHHH!

CHAPTER 4

THE CALL

When we emerge from the kitchen, me gently dripping and Milo clutching the lobster, Aunty Bindi, still in her dressing gown and rollers, sort of flops face down in despair onto the sofa, leaving an icky green stain on Mum's favourite cream velvet cushion. Mum calmly goes upstairs to steam the creases out of her outfit for tomorrow. Dad goes off to his study, asking no one in particular why things are never straightforward around here. As usual, no one answers him. And I suddenly realize **NOBODY** is in the least bit bothered that I have lobster wee **ALL OVER ME**!

As I look around for a towel or, even better,

an antibacterial wipe, I see Uncle Ricky slithering off into the marquee while staring intently at his phone screen. The twins have skulked off somewhere too.

Granny Jas marches up and down, muttering in a mixture of Hindi and English and tapping her head. I just **KNOW** there are some bad words in there. She mentions something about the greenhouse and saunters off, her white- and lemon-coloured sari billowing in the breeze. She's always in the greenhouse these days; I can't imagine what's so interesting about her hyacinths and herbs.

Granny Jas is my dad's mum and she's always lived with us. Granny has no teeth, **none at all**! That would be gross on anyone else but it's quite funny on Granny. She wears dentures when she remembers to, but sometimes leaves them in odd places. Like the time she left them on the side table in the living room, and when the telephone rang, Mum picked them up by accident!

When I was younger and had particularly tricky

school projects, Mum would tell Dad to help me. Dad would say, "Why don't you do it with Granny Jas, she'd enjoy that!" (Only because he didn't have a clue either.) One time we had to make a papier-mâché planet. The instructions said you needed plain flour and water. We didn't have any plain flour, but Granny Jas said chapati flour would be fine. "Same thing!" she announced gleefully.

I can tell you it was **NOT** the same thing and the result was crusty and crumpled. I was so **embarrassed**, but it was too late to start again so I had to take the chapati planet in. I tried to pass it off as a moon rock, but everyone laughed and my teacher, Mr Stern, was not happy at all. He thought I had done it as a joke, so I got a letter home.

Mum told off Dad and Dad told off Granny Jas. Granny reminded Dad that she is his mum and she would stop cooking for him if he said anything else!

Right now, guests are arriving and Aunty Suki ushers them into the marquee. It fills up really quickly and soon the guests are spilling out into the garden. Aunty Bindi disappears to get ready upstairs – no way will she let anyone see her with rollers and a green face. Milo sits behind the sofa, whispering to the lobster. After I splash water all over my face and scrub it raw with a flannel, then spray myself with some **eau de pew** from Mum's bathroom shelf, I go over and sit with him.

"I hope you're not making friends with him, Milo," I say in my best mum voice.

"He says his name's Larry." Milo smiles, stroking the lobster's hard, shiny shell. The lobster seems to like it.

"No, Milo!

Granny Jas is cooking him later. Remember, lobster curry!" I insist.

"She can't! I won't let her!" exclaims Milo, putting his arms protectively over the lobster. He tilts his head to the side as if listening. "He doesn't think it's fair that your dad wants to eat him. He says your dad should explore veganism."

I'm about to argue with Milo that the lobster couldn't possibly have said that, because, well, he's a lobster – but then the phone rings.

There's no one else in the living room now so I jump up and answer it, hoping it's not a relative who wants to talk to me in Hindi.

"**Why has the wedding not been cancelled as we instructed?**" The voice is muffled, like the person is talking through a thick scarf. It gives me the creeps.

"Who is this?" I demand.

"**You don't need to know that**."

I strain to hear if there are any clues as to where

the caller could be. There's a low humming and lots of background noise, like the person is in a crowded place. I think I hear music tinkling.

"**Just make sure the wedding is cancelled by seven o'clock this evening**."

"Where's Tony? How do I know you haven't thrown him over a cliff or hurt him?"

"**You don't. CANCEL THE WEDDING. OR ELSE**." And the line goes dead.

I hang up, my brain whirring. There was something strange about the phone call – apart from the obvious thing of it being from a kidnapper.

"Who was that? Your face has gone all weird," Milo says.

I look around, paranoid someone could be listening.

"It was the kidnapper. They said the wedding has to be cancelled by seven this evening. It's already three minutes and twenty-three seconds past one

now," I whisper. And then… "Can you hear that?"
I ask Milo.

"Hear what? Tell me more about what they said
on the phone."

I ignore Milo's question and head into the
kitchen. The back door is open and I step out into
the garden, closely followed by Milo, who's holding
the lobster. To the left of us, the back of the house juts
out and the marquee attached to it fills up most of the
space. Somewhere past it, I hear the sound again.

I look down to the far end of the garden, at the
row of tall trees which Milo quite often tries to climb.
He says it makes him feel in touch with nature –
except for that one time when he disturbed a wasps'
nest by accident. Wasps are not that friendly when
they think you're attacking them, apparently.

The rest of the garden is full of people chattering
and laughing. I walk past the marquee and down on
to the grass, listening for the sound. There it is again!

Tinkling music! It's coming from the front of the

house now. How is it moving around so much? I run quickly to the side gate and flip the latch to open it. Milo follows me into the alley and out to the front of our house – just as an ice-cream van goes chiming past.

"That's **the exact music** I heard in the background of the call from the kidnapper," I gasp. We both turn and look back at my house and then at each other.

"Does that mean…" begins Milo.

"The phone call must have come from **inside** the house."

"Are you **sure** someone here made that phone call, Neesh? Really? Surely it couldn't be someone from your own family. Why would any of your relatives want to kidnap Uncle Tony? Everyone is so nice! Do you think all this is making you a bit para?" Milo exclaims as we walk back through the alley and into the garden.

"I'm **paranoid** for good reason!" I hiss. "I told you – there might not be a wedding at all if we don't find Uncle Tony and whoever is trying to stop him marrying Aunty Bindi."

"Look, let's slow things down. Show me the note. It's probably just a joke." Milo pulls me to the end of the garden by the hedge where it's quieter. He places the lobster carefully near Mum's water feature, where it seems to enjoy the spray coming out of the fish statue's mouth.

Milo takes the note and holds it between thumb and forefinger, turning it this way and that. It's a shame I don't have a fingerprinting kit. I asked for one for my last birthday, but for some reason Mum didn't want me messing around with chemicals in the house. I don't know what her problem is – it was a total accident when I dyed the bath bright green with my home-made bath crystals. They were meant to be a present for Mum, but it went a bit wrong. I did try to remind her that it could be worse. I could always be getting into trouble, like the kids you see on telly (Aunty Bindi likes to watch the soaps, so I've reluctantly seen a few episodes). Anyway, Mum was not impressed with my argument.

Suddenly, we're interrupted.

"And what do you have there, hmm?"

Granny Jas pops her head over the hedge behind us and grins a gummy grin. She's forgotten to put her teeth in again. "Come on, tell Granny Jas what the big secret is." She peers over my shoulder at the note and narrows her eyes.

"Oh, just boring school stuff. You wouldn't be interested. Honestly, it's a **snore fest**." Milo smiles innocently at Granny Jas as he passes the note to me behind our backs.

Granny stares hard at us, first at Milo and then at me. "I see," she says slowly. "That is a pity. Well, if you ever want any help with your **snoring fest**..."

She goes back behind the hedge and we hear her shutting the greenhouse door firmly and locking it. Then she walks round past us and through the now quite large groups of guests in the garden to the kitchen, her sari pleats flicking out in front of her as she goes. "Don't forget, that lobster is your daddy's dinner, Anni," she calls over her shoulder. "I'll be getting my big thali ready now."

"What's a thali?" Milo asks worriedly.

"A big tray for putting food on," I answer.

The lobster's antennae quiver and Milo scoops him up protectively. Lobsters aren't really that cuddly though and one of its claws pokes him in the eye.

"So, we need a plan," I say, getting out the note and unscrunching it. "I think it's from someone we know, so we need to watch the family carefully at the mehndi party – look out for any suspicious behaviour and any reasons why someone might not want the wedding to go ahead. Then, once we've figured out who it could be, we can work out where they've hidden Tony. We'll save the wedding and, more importantly, there will **not be any drama**! We can't let on to Mum or Aunty Bindi that anything is wrong. So, whatever you do, just act **NORMAL.**"

"Yes, sir. I mean madam…I mean miss," says Milo.

"No, Milo, seriously, we have to be undercover, like spies."

Milo grins. "Yes, spies! We can have our own **Secret Spy Club**! I can be **Agent Double-Zero** and you can be **Agent Double-Double-Zero**. We can talk in code and I'll get my walkie-talkies from home! Maybe Larry can be Lieutenant Lobster, crusty cop! You'd like that, wouldn't you, Larry?" he coos at Larry the Lobster.

I sigh for the second time. This is going to be very hard work.

Just then Uncle Ricky appears from behind a tree, still with his phone in his hand, looking very shifty. What was he doing back there?

He notices us watching him. "I'm…um…just popping out. Tell your parents I'll be back later, will you? I've left the paper cups and plates in the kitchen that your mum wanted me to pick up." Then he practically sprints through the marquee and the house, towards the front door.

Milo and I look at each other and speak at exactly the same time: "We have to follow him!"

CHAPTER 6

THE KING

We run through the house after Uncle Ricky,
ignoring Aunty Suki yelling at us to **SLOW DOWN**.
We're going so fast we almost trip over Mindy and
Manny, who are lurking at the bottom of the
stairs.

"**Where** are you two going?" Mindy asks sweetly.

I turn to face her and force the biggest smile
I can. "Nowhere. Just popping out to check
something," I answer. My feet suddenly seem stuck
to the ground.

Manny smirks, barely looking up from his tablet.

"We have to go and check on my cat, Yasmine.
She's had a very difficult morning," Milo explains.

"Hmm, if you say so."
Mindy raises one tweezed
eyebrow. "I'll see you
later, Anisha. And don't
worry – if I see your mum
I'll be sure to tell her that
you're just 'checking on
the cat'."

And with that,
she and Manny stalk
upstairs.

"Haven't they got anything better to do than sit
around being **WEIRD and SCARY**?" asks Milo.

"I don't know," I sigh. "But we haven't got time to worry about them now. We need to catch up with Uncle Ricky. What if he leads us to a clue – or even straight to Uncle Tony?"

I take Mum's straw gardening hat for my own head from the pegs by the door and plonk Dad's golfing cap on top of Milo's mop of ginger curls – the best disguises I can come up with at short notice.

We peek out of the front door carefully; the street is quiet. Uncle Ricky is walking up the road. Strange – he never walks anywhere. This could be a **clue**, we'd better investigate! We slip outside, looking around us all the time. Mustaf is ferreting around in the boot of the limo. Luckily, he doesn't look up and we slide past unnoticed.

"We have to follow at a distance and blend into our surroundings like chameleons," Milo whispers, glancing at me sideways while pulling the golf cap further down over his eyes. I'm not sure he can see anything except his feet now and I grab his arm just in time to steer him round a lamp post.

"Did you know, **a chameleon's spit is 400 times more sticky than a human's**?" he goes on.

"No, Milo, I didn't know that." I smile. I'm used to him telling me animal facts when he's nervous.

As we follow Uncle Ricky in silence I think about what possible reasons he might have to want to stop the wedding. I know he and Uncle Tony don't always get on, but what could he have against Aunty Bindi? What could he have to gain? A series of possibilities flash through my mind:

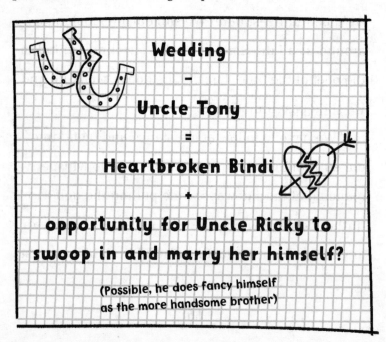

Wedding

-

Uncle Tony

=

Heartbroken Bindi

+

opportunity for Uncle Ricky to swoop in and marry her himself?

(Possible, he does fancy himself as the more handsome brother)

OR:

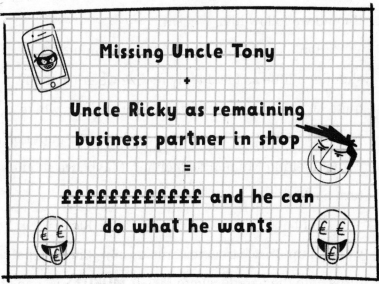

Missing Uncle Tony

+

Uncle Ricky as remaining business partner in shop

=

£££££££££££ and he can do what he wants

Just then, Milo tugs on my arm to get my attention. Uncle Ricky is slowing down. Milo and I pause at the corner of the street as he **disappears** from view. I poke my head around the corner, cautiously angling Mum's straw hat so it casts a shadow over my face. Uncle Ricky is walking down Brick Street towards the market. He **vanishes** under the cover of one of the stalls.

"What's going on? Let me look too!" Milo pokes

his head round below mine. "Where's he going? Should we follow him, Neesh?"

"I don't know, Milo, let me think a minute." I shudder a little as I suddenly realize we are actually quite far away from my house. No one knows where we've gone, and we're not supposed to just wander off without telling Mum or Dad either. Maybe we should turn back?

I peer back around the corner. Uncle Ricky is walking up Brick Street towards us now, but then he turns onto the parade where **MEGA MOBILES** is, one of the shops he runs with Uncle Tony. He's using both hands to drag a large wheelie bag along. What could be in there?

"Come on, Milo, we have to follow that bag!"

Mega Mobiles has a huge glass front with hundreds of mobile phones on display that reflect the sunlight. Uncle Ricky heads inside, stops to speak to one of his staff and then goes into the back of the shop, still dragging the wheelie bag behind him.

Uncle Ricky
+
mysterious black bag **?**
=
Time to investigate

"Come on, Milo, we have to see what he's up to. What if he's got Uncle Tony tied up in the back?" Any thoughts I had about turning back are gone and I know we have to go into that shop.

"Do you really think so, Neesh? I don't know… Maybe we should call the police or your mum and dad?"

"No time for that! Come on, **QUICK**! Let's at least see what's going on before we call anyone. It's busy in there. If we're quick, the sales people won't notice us – we can sneak past."

We walk into the **gleaming white shop**. There are plenty of customers keeping the staff busy, so we slowly edge our way round the store, careful not to attract any attention. Milo nods as I pretend to point out phones while we make our way, centimetre by centimetre, to the door at the back of the shop.

We wait and watch for an opportunity to go through. A customer calls the manager over to the other side of the room – this is it, we can go...

"Can I help you with anything, young people?" A sales lady stands in front of us, blocking the way.

I think fast. "My friend here, he really needs the toilet."

"This is not a public restroom, young lady."

"**I CAN'T HOLD IT!**" Milo joins in, realizing what I'm up to.

"He really needs to go," I say. "I don't think you want a puddle on the floor. My Uncle Tony owns this shop, so I know where to go and he'd definitely let us go back there and use the toilet. I could call him if you like, but I'm not sure he'd want to be disturbed the day before his **wedding**," I say, crossing my fingers behind my back.

The lady frowns at me, thinking for a minute. "Um, well I suppose as you're family it's okay. But be quick now, I'll be checking in **five minutes**."

"Thank you so much!" we both say and race through the door to the back of the shop, Milo still hopping about like he needs a wee.

"You can stop now, Milo, she's not looking any more."

"Oh, well I actually do need the toilet now – it was all that talk about needing to go!"

"You'll have to hold it!"

There's the sound of music as we approach the office. Weird grown-up music, I've heard it before somewhere.

"I know this music!" Milo claps. "It's the King!"

"The King?" I'm confused for a minute and then I realize he means **the King of Rock and Roll** – Uncle Tony's favourite musician ever! "Elvis!*"

The song is blaring out from the office and I can hear what sounds like someone crooning along with it: "**Oooooooooooh ooo, yeah yeah, mm mm, mm, mm, yay, yay, yaaaaaaaaay yeah!**"

Milo covers his ears and whispers, "Whoever that is, they really shouldn't sing!"

I nod in agreement. But can this have anything to do with Uncle Tony being kidnapped? I wonder.

The office door is slightly ajar so I push it gently, just enough so I can see through the crack. Then I kind of wish I hadn't looked...

You know sometimes you see something you really wish you could **UN**see? Well, this is one of those times.

✪★✩☆★✪★✩☆★✩☆★✪☆★✩☆✪★✪★✩☆★✩✩★✪★✩

* Elvis Presley was the King of Rock and Roll music in the 1950s and 60s. He's probably one of the most famous people of all time actually.

Uncle Ricky, dressed in a white jumpsuit with gold and purple gems all along the sleeves, is wiggling around the room, his extra-wide gem-encrusted collar flapping about as he shimmies across the office. He stops by the mirror on the wall and runs a brush

through his hair, making it puff up into a quiff. He pulls out his phone and takes a selfie, then practises curling his top lip in the mirror. I suddenly notice our gobsmacked faces are in the reflection too. Oh no, he's seen us!

"**WHAT THE...?!!** What are you two doing here?" he yells.

I think quickly. Do we run and risk him phoning my mum? Or do we stay and try to talk our way out of it? After all, Uncle Ricky might still know something about Uncle Tony's kidnap.

"**Oh, hi, Uncle Ricky!**" I say brightly. "We came to see if you needed any help preparing for the wedding. Mum sent us out for a few things and we were going past and thought we'd, you know, be helpful."

Uncle Ricky eyes us both suspiciously. I don't think he believes my story for a second. Milo gulps and stares at the floor.

"Hmm. Well, no, I don't need any help, but it's very thoughtful of you to offer," Ricky says.

"That's okay. I...erm...like your outfit, Uncle Ricky. Are you going to a **fancy-dress party**?" I ask.

Uncle Ricky looks pleased that I like his outfit and then **annoyed** that I've said the wrong thing.

"Well, you two can talk! What's with the funny hats? Actually, if you must know, it's a **surprise** for my brother and your Aunty Bindi," he huffs.

"Oh, a surprise! That sounds **amazingly clever**!" I say, trying more flattery to win him over and hopefully get another clue.

"Well, yes, I suppose it **IS** clever. Tony will never expect it," chuckles Uncle Ricky. "I'm going to give a surprise performance at the wedding reception tomorrow! Tony's been a massive Elvis fan ever since we were kids. My mate Dave from the market got hold of the outfit for me and this too." He points to the open wheelie bag in the corner of the room. Inside is a **huge glitter ball**! "I only just got it so I thought I'd give it a whirl." He grins.

Milo and I look at each other and I have to stop myself from laughing.

"What's so funny?" Uncle Ricky frowns.

"Nothing! I think it's great, Uncle Ricky. That sounds so interesting. Please tell us more about your performance!" I say quickly.

"Well, this was our parents' favourite Elvis song,

back in the day, and Tony and I used to dance around the living room to it when we were boys. He does a good Elvis impression, you know!" Uncle Ricky smiles at the memory.

I decide to push for information while he's in a good mood. "So, have you spoken to Uncle Tony today then? He must be **VERY** excited for the big day. I know Aunty Bindi is!"

"Actually, no. I haven't seen or spoken to him since yesterday, now you mention it. I tried him this morning, but he never called me back. I expect he's busy preparing, or he'll have been with **the twins**, I imagine. I think they've been giving him a bit of trouble over this wedding, so he's been trying to reassure them. They miss their mum, of course. Terrible shame about her being so far away in **Bollywood**. Anyway, I'm sure I'll see Tony this evening at his house. I'm the best man, you know! Now, you two should run along, it's half past one already. I'm sure your mother will be wondering where you have got to, Anni. Plus, I have to practise my moves!" He flicks his collar up and winks at us.

We say goodbye and obediently walk back out through the shop.

"Does that mean Uncle Ricky isn't the kidnapper then?" Milo asks, rubbing his head as we step back onto the street.

"The only thing Uncle Ricky is guilty of is **crimes against fashion and music**." I sigh. "Come on, we'd better do as he said and go home. Hopefully no one has noticed we've gone."

As we walk home I can't help but start to panic. We're no closer to finding Uncle Tony and we have no idea where to look next!

When we get back to Jewel Street, our nosy neighbour, Mr Bogof from **number 62**, is standing outside his house. He's dressed in a waistcoat and trousers with a funny neck tie – I **think** it's called a **cravat**. Dad sometimes wears one when he has fancy work dinners. Mr Bogof always dresses like this, though, even when he doesn't seem to be going anywhere. We pull our hats down over our faces to try to disguise ourselves as we go past him, but no such luck.

"**Oi, you two, come here**. I've got a word or three for you."

"**Oh, hi,** Mr Bogof, how are you?" I try to keep my voice light and carry on walking, but he blocks our path.

"Don't you '**oh, hi!**' me, **young missy**! I know exactly what's going on over there." He points down the street at our house and waggles his finger.

For a second, I think he actually knows about Uncle Tony being kidnapped. I shuffle nervously. "You do?"

"Oh, yes! All the coming and going from **number 52**! Cars blocking up the road, the noise all day and night, those **two WEIRD-LOOKING kids** always in black on their phones – they were out front earlier making the street look untidy. I'm not stupid – I know what's going on!" He taps the side of his head firmly.

I realize he doesn't know anything about Uncle Tony. And we don't have time for this!

"I'm sorry, Mr Bogof, I don't know what you mean and we **REALLY** have to get home. There's nothing to worry about, it's just a **family wedding**. It'll be over after tomorrow." I start to walk away, hoping he doesn't follow us.

"You'll see! No good can come of family gatherings! You'll see! That's why I live alone. **You'll see I'm right!**" Mr Bogof's voice echoes after us all the way down the street.

CHAPTER 7

MEHNDI MAYHEM

With Mr Bogof's warning still ringing in my ears,
I check my watch when we get in. It's already forty-
seven minutes and three, I mean four, seconds past
one. The mehndi party is starting and the house is
overflowing with people. The kidnapper's threat
replays in my mind: **You have until 7 p.m.
tonight. OR ELSE!!!!** We don't have long left,
just over five hours.

I look around, desperately hoping for a clue about
where or who to investigate next. Aunties, uncles,
distant relatives I've never met and friends of the
family are all here to wish Aunty Bindi well for her
big day. Cousins who haven't seen each other for

80

years hug and laugh together. I know that secretly some of them don't even like each other – they grin through gritted teeth. Aunty is, of course, **loving** it all. She adores being the centre of attention and has her best sparkling smile on display, as well as a bright yellow-and-pink sari. She'll be so embarrassed and upset if there's no Uncle Tony tomorrow. The thought makes my tummy turn upside down.

Milo and I squeeze past all the people and head into the kitchen, which is filled with the smell of spices and fried food. The counter is piled high with all my favourite treats – Granny has been cooking all week. Bowls of sticky **gelebi** and a small mountain of colourful blocks of **barfi**, which are my favourite because they taste like fudge, make my mouth water and I realize I haven't eaten since this morning. Pots of curry bubble away on the stove, making clouds of hot steam. On the edge of the counter lies a pile of silver tubes. I'm not sure what those are for.

Just then Dad sneaks in. He's clearly hiding from

Mum because he puts his finger to his lips when he sees us.

"Hello, kids," he whispers. "What mischief are you up to in here then?"

"Not much, Dad. Just hiding from all the relatives and eating some food while Granny's not looking – like you!" I joke, trying to peer past Dad into the garden at two guests who look like they're whispering to each other. **Maybe they're the kidnappers!** My brain is whirring while I try to keep smiling.

"Um, ah, well..." Dad scratches his head and chuckles as he realizes he's been **rumbled**.

"It's yummy," Milo says with a mouthful of **samosa**.

We all grab a handful of sticky **gelebi** and start stuffing our faces, just as Granny walks in. In a rush to hide what we're doing, Dad accidentally knocks the silver tubes onto the floor. As I crouch down to help gather them up, a strong smell shoots right up my nostrils. It's like medicine and mint and something that I **KNOW** I've smelled before, but can't put my finger on...

"Hmm, and what is going on here then?" Granny frowns.

"Nothing, Granny," I say, in my best "**good child**" voice. I have found from previous experience that if you've been caught doing something wrong the best course of action is:

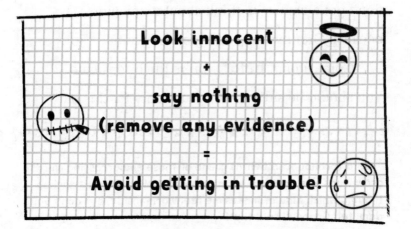

"Yes, and the sticky mess around your mouth is 'nothing', I suppose!" Granny puts her hand on her hip. Oops, I forgot to wipe away the evidence.

"Did you need something from in here, **Mummiji**?" Dad stutters. (He always calls her "**Mummiji**" when he's done something wrong.)

"Hmm? Oh, I just wanted the mehndi tubes. We're getting ready to make Bindi all **beautiful**!"

"Ah well, here they are." Dad hands the silver tubes to Granny, smiling sweetly. As she walks past me I get a whiff of that smell again. What **IS** that? I **KNOW** I've smelled it somewhere else today, but I don't get a chance to think about it any more because Granny turns and grabs my hand.

"Come along, **beta***, you're the bridesmaid. You should be sitting with your aunty for this bit."

1★☆☆✿☆✰★✿☆✿★✿☆✿★☆✿★✿☆★✿☆★✿✰✿★✿★☆☆✿☆✿★✿✰☆✿

* Beta (pronounced behta) is one of those embarrassing words grown-ups use instead of my name. It does mean "darling" though, which kind of makes me feel warm inside, but don't you dare tell Granny I said that!

"Oh...er...I just need to pop upstairs, Granny."
I panic. I can't sit down and do nothing – we'll never find Uncle Tony if I keep getting stopped. All these celebrations will be pointless if there's no groom!

"No, no time for that, come on, beta, they're waiting to start."

Reluctantly, Milo and I follow Granny out to the packed marquee. I sit down to the side of Mum and Milo crouches behind me. Granny gives the tubes to the lady who is going to apply the mehndi. Mum, Aunty Bindi and Aunty Suki are sitting on big colourful pillows on the floor of the marquee together. You'd never tell they are sisters; they all look so different. Mum is all wavy-haired and free-spirited, calm and carefree. Bindi is big hair, big heart and big mouth – she always speaks her mind. Suki has a sleek bob, neat and shiny. I wonder who I'll turn out like when I'm older...

I think about when I was younger and everyone said I looked so much like Bindi. People used to think I was her daughter when we were out together. Although that was probably because she used to dress us in matching outfits – **hot pink** is not a colour I would pick now! But still, she looked after me a lot when I was little. Maybe that's why I feel like I need to make sure no one ruins her big day. I can't even imagine how upset she'll be if Uncle Tony isn't there for the wedding. She's been looking forward to marrying him so much. **I can't let her down.**

Sitting around Mum and my aunties are all the women in the family. Some are singing old Indian wedding songs, others are chatting amongst themselves as they wait to watch Aunty Bindi having her mehndi put on. Later they'll have mehndi applied too, but the bride is the **most important** and is always **decorated first**.

The mehndi lady kneels on the sheeted floor in front of Aunty Bindi and squeezes mehndi from the silver tubes into her special silver cone, which she uses to draw the pattern on. She puts two whole tubefuls into the cone and then starts to draw the **swirly** designs on Aunty Bindi's outstretched arms. That **WEIRD** smell is here again, and it gets **STRONGER** and **STRONGER** until it stings my nostrils. In a split second I know exactly what it is.

I turn and whisper to Milo, "Can you smell that? I couldn't place it before, but it's that heat rub

Granny Jas uses on her gammy leg. Oh no! What if a tube of that stuff got mixed up with the mehndi? We have to do something!"

Granny Jas's heat rub is the **SMELLIEST**, pongiest, most pungent stuff I've ever smelled. It's a mix of hospitals, medicines, spices and really-strong-mints-that-are-so-minty-they-tickle-your-nose, but times ten! Granny Jas rubs the stinky ointment into her gammy foot twice a day and it does help her, but still – the smell!

Also, I got some in my eye once (I'd put some on my finger just to see what it was like and then forgot to wash my hands and rubbed my eye) and it stings like you're on fire! So if I'm right:

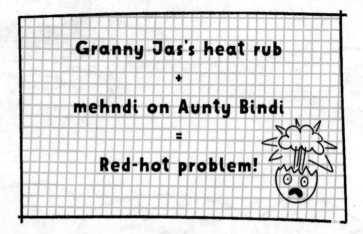

Granny Jas's heat rub

+

mehndi on Aunty Bindi

=

Red-hot problem!

Bang on cue:

"That's weird. I smell something strange," Aunty Bindi says.

"It'll just be the henna," says the mehndi lady as she carries on piping the design onto Bindi's arms, although even she is starting to frown.

"No, I think she's right. That's not the smell of mehndi. It's a medicinal smell," says Mum.

"Oh! I think something's wrong! Should my arms be **tingling** like this?" asks Aunty Bindi in a worried voice.

"Hmm, not really," says the mehndi lady, also scrunching up her nose as the smell gets stronger.

As I scan the crowd and look through to the living room, I see Mindy and Manny watching from the doorway.

"**OHHH, NOOO!** This doesn't feel good!" Aunty Bindi squeals, and I look back to see she has gone bright red. Her skin is covered in **big fire-**

engine-red blotches where the mehndi has been painted on.

"**GET IT OFF!**" she yells. "It's burning me!"

Things happen really fast then. The marquee erupts into a muddle of shouting and wailing and screeching. Aunty Suki yells at Dad to "**DO SOMETHING!**" Dad shouts at everyone to "**KEEP CALM!**" Granny Jas tells Aunty Bindi not to be a drama queen – which **DOES NOT HELP**. Mum tries to get Aunty Bindi to "**breathe through the pain**", which seems to make Bindi really angry and she says some bad words in Hindi. Mum goes a bit red in the face and mumbles that she was only trying to help. Everyone is yelling at everyone else, guests are shouting "**helpful**" suggestions and just as it's all getting a bit out of hand, Manny and Mindy come running in with a big bucket of water and tip its entire contents over Aunty Bindi.

SPLASH!

There is a stunned silence as Aunty Bindi gets
to her feet, soaked from head to toe, with the brown
gooey mehndi dripping off her. Bella the dog trots
over, takes one sniff and runs away yelping. I put my
head in my hands and wonder for the millionth time
why my family can't just be normal.

CHAPTER 8

SUPER-SIZED SAMOSAS AND GENETICALLY MODIFIED CUCUMBERS

After the whole mehndi/heat-rub drama, the grown-ups try to mop up and Mum wafts one of her aromatherapy candles around. Aunty Suki takes Aunty Bindi out to the garden to hose her down. The poor mehndi lady is apologizing to anyone who will listen and telling them she just doesn't understand what could have happened. She offers to do some mehndi on some of the other ladies but they try to distract her with a cup of tea instead.

Milo and I hide out upstairs in my room. Milo is

making Larry the
lobster a rock pool
out of an old
plastic lid and
some rocks from
the garden and
keeping him
cool with a
damp cloth all
the while trying
to speak lobsterish.

I take the chance to look out of the bedroom
window over the back garden and observe the
guests. There must be **at least** a hundred people
in our house and garden now.

"It's someone down there, Milo. **I just know
it is!** But who?"

"Let's think about it, Neesh. Do that analysing
thing you do – you're good at that."

I get a bit hot in the cheeks then. I didn't know

Milo thought I was good at being logical – I didn't think he listened to me half of the time. But he's right, I just have to think logically and get there by a process of elimination. I grab a piece of paper and a pen from my bedside drawer.

"Okay."

I start to write:

LIST OF SUSPECTS

- **Uncle Ricky – too busy being Elvis to have masterminded a kidnap plot, plus he wants the wedding to go ahead so he can have his moment in the spotlight.**
- **The twins – they have the alibi of being at boarding school, Aunty Bindi said that they didn't arrive here until this morning, plus they just tried to help Aunty Bindi during the heat-rub disaster.**

"What about that neighbour of ours?" Milo suggests as he takes the paper and pen from me and writes:

> Mr Bogof – doesn't like his street being disturbed by the wedding. Could have taken Uncle Tony so that the wedding celebrations stop.

"That seems a bit unlikely, Milo. How did you come up with that theory?" I say.

"I dunno, anything's possible!" He shrugs.

"Milo, be serious!" I take the paper and pen back.

"Well, who do **you** think it could be then?"

I think for a second, remembering something Mum was talking about last week, and write:

> - **Tony's mum and dad – don't approve of the wedding. Overheard saying they thought Bindi was like a walking, talking dolly.**

"Yeah, but wouldn't they just take him away and not say anything? Why would they send a kidnap note and make an anonymous call?"

Milo has a point.

"Whoever is behind this appears to be playing some kind of game. It's like they're testing us. They're enjoying watching us run around looking for Tony."

"Do you really think they're watching us?" Milo worries.

"Well if it's someone here then, yes, they probably are, Milo. I just wish I could figure out who would want the wedding to be **CANCELLED**!"

Then I realize something – something

ABSOLUTELY TERRIBLY COMPLETELY AWFUL.

"Oh no! Do you realize who we haven't put on the list, Milo? Granny Jas! It was her medicine that got mixed up with Bindi's mehndi. **AND** she has been really secretive about whatever is in her greenhouse over the last couple of days."

I think hard. Something comes back to me. The note! Why didn't I think of it before? I pull it from my pocket. "**Smell this!**" I say, pushing the paper under Milo's nose.

"What the...urgh...what's that? It's like...um... it's like, you know, medicine and mint and..."

I smell the note again myself and jump up. "**Granny Jas's heat rub!** I knew I'd smelled that smell before. I just couldn't remember where!"

"But, Neesh, **your granny**?"

"I know, Milo, it sounds **BONKERS**! But right now it's the best lead we've got. We **have** to get inside that

greenhouse. The wedding could depend on it.
We need to find out what Granny is hiding – for all
we know, Uncle Tony could be trapped in there with
some genetically modified giant cucumbers!"

We leave Larry the lobster scuttling around his
rock pool in my room and make our way downstairs
and through the living room, trying not to get
trapped by talkative relatives or, worse still, Aunty
Rupi from Leicester, who always likes to give sloppy
kisses. **URGH.**

As I get to the far end of the living room I spot
Granny in the marquee, trying to force-feed Aunty
Bindi's work friends some fried green chillies,
a delicacy if you're used to spicy foods, but they
look quite scared. She's happily occupied, so I tell
Milo to keep an eye on her and I sneak out the
back door.

I run down the garden to the greenhouse. I'm
glad it's slightly hidden away from the main bit of
the garden by the big hedge. Granny always says

it's her getaway from us lot. I press my face against the window. The glass is misty and plants fill the shelves, so I can't see much from the outside. I try the door but it's locked. Uncle Tony **MUST** be in there! Granny has found the perfect place to hide him! I have to get him out!

"Looking for something, beta?" Granny makes me jump, sneaking up on me like that!

"Um, no, Granny. I was just looking for a place to hide out, you know, away from all the crazy family stuff." I smile weakly.

"Oh yes, I know what you mean. Well, the greenhouse is always locked, beta, you know I don't like anyone disturbing my work in there. Come on, I'll dish you up a samosa. You love my super-sized samosas." And with that she guides me by the shoulders, away from the greenhouse and back towards the house.

CATASTROPHIC COSMOS! I have to get hold of the key to the greenhouse and I have to do it soon!

CHAPTER 9

GOTCHA, GRANNY!

Having foiled my attempt to get into the greenhouse, Granny escorts me back into the kitchen. Strangely, Mustaf is in there. I don't think I've ever seen him eating actual food, but when we walk in he jumps and quickly puts his hand behind his back. He nods at Granny and goes to leave, but not before I see there's a napkin stuffed with samosas scrunched up in his hand. He shoves it in his pocket as he strides away.

I look around for a way to distract Granny – I **REALLY** need to get the key to the greenhouse.

Just then Milo pops his head round the kitchen door from the living room. "Oh, there you are,

Neesh! What are you doing?" he asks innocently.

"Hi, Granny Jas, I was just admiring your greenhouse earlier and saying to Anisha that I'd love to see inside. I've always fancied learning how to grow things."

"Being green-fingered cannot be taught and **NO ONE** is allowed in my greenhouse. Do you understand?" Granny snaps and storms off into the living room, leaving behind the smell of sweet spices and foot cream.

"Oh, I see what you mean!" sighs Milo. "She **IS** acting very auspicious. And why did she think I wanted green fingers?"

"You mean Granny is being **SUS**picious, Milo, and yes, she is. I'm going to get inside that greenhouse and I'm doing it right now."

"But the greenhouse is always locked, you said."

"Yes, but I know where Granny keeps the key. We just have to be really careful not to get caught! Go and stand by the greenhouse and wait for me."

A few minutes later I emerge from the kitchen with the key and a very yellow hand.

"What happened to you, Neesh? Did you get it?" Milo asks as I walk over to him at the end of the garden. "Your hand is yellow by the way."

"She keeps the key in the turmeric tin. Of all the spices she could hide it in, she chooses the one that stains everything it touches. I'll have a yellow hand for days!"

"Didn't your granny say it was lucky when they covered Bindi in it yesterday?" Milo remembers, laughing.

"Trust you to remember that, Milo. Now **shush**! You just keep a lookout. Granny could go to get her key at any time, so we have to be quick."

I put the key in the lock and turn it slowly. There's a click and the door swings open.

We look behind us and then making sure no one is watching we both step into the greenhouse. It's quieter in here and hot. The smell of herbs and plants is overpowering. I'm just about to start looking under crates and pots when…

"**EH YEH KYA HAI**, what do you two think you are doing in here?"

I gulp and turn around to face Granny Jas. I think about coming up with an excuse, but my mind is blank. There's no going back now. My heart thumps and my hands are clammy as I hear myself saying, "Granny, I know you've kidnapped Uncle Tony and that you put your heat rub in the mehndi tubes and that you want to stop the wedding. Now **WHERE IS HE**, just tell me!"

Granny looks at me for a second, then squints her eyes and creases up her face. I wait for her to say something; to deny it; to tell me off or something. But she doesn't. She laughs! **Can you believe it?** She is actually laughing. I've just uncovered her dastardly plan and she's laughing!

"Am I understanding you properly, beta? You think I want to stop the wedding? Why would I want to do that? It's such a **khushi*** time for our family. Where did you get such a funny idea?"

"You pushed a note through the front door saying Uncle Tony had been kidnapped and I thought it was Uncle Ricky at first but it wasn't and I've been trying to think who else it could be and then I realized." My hands are itching, my face is all hot, and suddenly I'm not so certain about all this but I keep going. "That stinky heat rub in the mehndi was **YOURS**, Granny, you know it was."

"Yes, it was, but anyone could have taken it. Do you think I would hurt Bindi like that?" Granny steps towards me.

"Don't come any closer, Granny, I MEAN IT!" I raise my voice but Granny just chuckles louder.

"The note smelled of that heat rub you use too

***

***** Did you know there's a famous Hindi film called KHABI KHUSHI, KHABIE GHAM (SOMETIMES WE'RE HAPPY, SOMETIMES WE'RE SAD). Aunty Bindi sings the song from it all the time – badly! Khushi means happy, which ironically is not what our neighbours are when Aunty Bindi is singing.

AND you wouldn't let anyone in the greenhouse. What are you hiding in here, if it's not Uncle Tony?" I say more boldly, looking around but not seeing anything more than fruit and herbs...and a sheet covering something large in the corner.

"Wait! What's that? **AHA!** What's this then?" I march over triumphantly to the weirdly-shaped lump and pull the sheet off, revealing...not Uncle Tony but – a mango tree!?!

"It's my mango tree, of course! The annual community fruit-growing competition is next month! I've been growing that tree for three years and this is the first year it's given me any fruit. I can't have any of my rivals peeking, can I? Especially that Mrs Kumar from number 23! You know she's Tony's great-aunty, don't you? I half suspected he's been trying to spy on my mangoes for her, always asking questions about my greenhouse."

Granny chuckles. "Oh, **beta**, you do tickle Granny's funny bone! I promise you I haven't been trying to stop the wedding. But now I have a question for you. What is this about a note and that **daft donkey** Tony being missing?"

I feel a bit silly then and realize how unlikely it is
that Granny is the kidnapper. I see that a scientist
wouldn't have got so carried away with one theory
and no real evidence. So I take another deep breath
and I tell Granny all about the note and Uncle
Ricky's **dodgy dancing** and the phone call from the
kidnapper and how we're running out of time to find
Uncle Tony.

Granny listens, nodding and frowning. "Are you
sure about this, beta, it does sound a little—"

"You don't believe me, do you?" I interrupt her,
disappointed.

"I didn't say that, did I? But it could be a joke,
no?" Granny touches my shoulder. "Come on,
we can sort this out together, **saath saath*** and
maybe we don't tell your mother or Bindi about
this just yet."

✮★✩☆★✮✮★✩✩★★✩✩★✮✩★★✩✩★★✩✮★✮✩★✩✩✮✩★✮☆✩

*** Saath saath means together. Granny Jas is always there when
I need her. I can't believe I thought she could be the kidnapper!**

So we make a plan. It's already seventeen minutes to three.

Granny says she'll go and watch the guests and see if she can spot anything suspicious. "If I were you, though, I'd start with that chauffeur, Mustaf. Have you seen how many of my samosas he took with him to the car? I know he's a big man, but what if he has someone **ELSE** he needs to feed out there?"

Now I think about it, Granny is right! Mustaf has been fishing about in the boot of the limo ever since he got here, but I haven't seen him bring in one item to do with the wedding yet. What if it's not wedding stuff in the boot, but **UNCLE TONY**?

WOW! Granny Jas is really good at this detective stuff!

We might still be able to figure it out before seven p.m. and **save the wedding**...although we have only just over four hours left, which is not that long. We have to find Uncle Tony, we just **HAVE** to.

The thought of Aunty Bindi all dressed for her wedding with **NO GROOM** is just too awful.

We decide we can't risk the kidnapper phoning the house again, so we unplug the house phone from its socket. Milo goes off to try and get Bindi's mobile phone too and hide it somewhere – and I head off to find mysterious Mustaf!

CHAPTER 10

MUSTAF AND THE NOSY NEIGHBOUR

Milo races into the marquee to try and get hold of Aunty Bindi's phone without being seen. Meanwhile I go to the front window, which looks out over the street. Mustaf is not by the car. **Great,** I think, **now's our chance to inspect the limo**.

"**ANISHA!**" comes a roar from across the room. "Come and talk to your favourite old cousin twice removed."

I close my eyes, take a deep breath and look in the direction of the voice. It's Dad's aunty's son's son (or something like that), Akshay. He is loud and obnoxious, runs a hardware store, and he wears this really strong aftershave – and a lot of it. It's called something like **IL STENCHO** for men.

"Hi, **Paji**.*" I try not to breathe in as my distant cousin comes swaying over.

"Enjoying the celebrations, are we? It'll be your turn soon!" he jokes and ruffles my hair like I'm a little kid. So annoying!.

"Er…I'm only ten, Paji," I say, composing myself. I think about telling him I have no plans to ever get married and would rather get a dog, but decide

---

* Paji means brother, even though Akshay's not my brother. Mum likes us to be respectful to our elders, so I have to call him Paji. All very confusing and super-annoying.

it's probably not something he'd understand.

He continues to talk, not particularly to me, but to the room in general. I glance around for Milo but he must still be trying to hide Bindi's phone.

"I was saying to Tony's twins only yesterday when they popped into the shop that you kids should come and work with me in your school holidays. I could teach you a thing or two about **DIY**. For example, did you know—"

Luckily before Akshay can tell me his ten most interesting **DIY facts**, Milo comes and rescues me, pretending Mum wants my help.

"Phew, thanks, Milo! I thought I was going to have to **FAKE-FAINT** or something to get out of there!" I whisper as we sneak out of the living room. "Did you manage to hide Bindi's phone?"

"Yes. I put it in your room under the bed with Larry the lobster and his rock pool. Hopefully he won't make any long-distance phone calls on it," Milo replies.

We creep outside and sneak over to the limo, ducking down as a police car goes by. The street is quiet after that, so I crawl round to the boot of the limo and listen for any sounds. There's a rustling noise and a soft thud.

"**Something's moving in there!**" I whisper to Milo.

"**OMG!** Do you think Mustaf has locked himself in the boot?" Milo exclaims.

"No, Milo! I think he's locked Uncle Tony in there. Remember? That's why we came out here! We only talked about it two minutes ago!"

"Oh, yeah, that's right. Sorry, got distracted. Look there's a hole in the boot, he must have drilled it so your uncle can breathe in there." Milo presses one eye against the hole. "It's a bit too dark to see though."

"Quick, help me open the boot before someone comes. Look, if we push together we might just..."

So I push and Milo pushes; we **HUFF** and **PUFF**,

and Milo's face turns a funny colour, but it's no good. The boot is locked.

"What are we going to do? Mustaf could come back any second," Milo hisses.

Before I can answer I hear, "**OI, YOU!** With the beard! Yes, you!"

Milo and I look at each other. I even touch my face. Is he talking to us?

I peek my head under the car and see Mr Bogof's smart trousers and shiny brown brogues. Next to them are Mustaf's black work shoes. Uh-oh. There's nowhere for us to go without being seen; we'll have to stay put.

Mr Bogof continues in his annoying **I'm better than you** voice. "Yes, I'm talking to you, sir. Do you know who I am? Clearly, you do not. I am the head of the **Jewel Street neighbourhood watch**. It is my duty to inform you that you, sir, are in breach of **code 142: loitering and perpetrating suspicious behaviour.** I have been observing you

and I have reason to believe you are in possession
of illegal goods in the boot of that vehicle. I will have
to ask—"

But Mr Bogof doesn't get to finish, because
Mustaf, still silent, is standing face-to-face (well
more like end-of-beard to forehead) with Mr Bogof,
and is now proceeding to lift him bodily into the air.

Milo squeals with excitement. This is **REAL
ACTION**! Who knows what Mustaf is capable of?
I feel I should rescue Mr Bogof, but a part of me just
really wants to see what happens next.

"**Put me down this instant!**" Mr Bogof
sputters, as his waistcoat flaps in the breeze.

Mustaf says nothing but does not put him down.
Instead he starts to walk with big heavy strides. Mr
Bogof's head seems to **boing** with every step. I worry
it will fall off. He looks terrified and is **YELPING**.
Mustaf is staring straight ahead, still not saying
a word. A crowd has gathered now – inquisitive
neighbours have come out of their houses to see

Mr Bogof get a taste of his own medicine. They watch gleefully as he is carried down the street.

As Mustaf reaches Mr Bogof's house, he looks up at it. It's the same as all the houses on Jewel Street, nothing special about it. The only thing that is different is Mr Bogof's security system. He's very proud of it. When he had it installed he sent a note round to all the neighbours, inviting them for a demonstration. Nobody turned up.

The security system is made up of several cameras on the front of the house, which are angled in all directions. There is also an emergency **siren** on the top of the house, in addition to a burglar **alarm**.

Mustaf looks at the cowering Mr Bogof in his grasp and lifts him even higher. I wonder if he might be getting ready to throw him. But he doesn't throw him. Instead he hooks him onto one of his security cameras and leaves him there. Mustaf clears his throat and I hear him speak for the first time ever, in the most surprising and squeakiest voice you can imagine.

"Now you can watch the **WHOLE**
neighbourhood."

At first the crowd remain
quiet and still –
probably shocked at
the squeak – but
then they go
wild, clapping
and cheering
and slapping
Mustaf on the
back (carefully...
they don't want to
end up hooked up
somewhere too).

Mr Bogof is helpless to do anything except hang
there, swinging his arms and legs in protest and
shouting at the whole street to get him down this
instant. No one does, of course.

I turn back to Milo. "We don't have long. Mustaf will come back any minute. We'll have to pick the lock."

"Do you even know how to do that, Neesh?" Milo looks at me, unconvinced.

"I might do – I've seen enough movies."

Just then it goes very dark, like the sun is being blocked out by the moon. Oh no, wait…that isn't the moon. Unless the moon is Mustaf-shaped. **UH-OH!**

Mustaf looms over us, eyes bulging, nostrils flaring and moustache quivering.

I think fast. "**AHA**," I say, pointing my finger at him, even though my mouth is suddenly very dry and someone is playing the drums in my chest.

"Have you lost your mind?" Milo whispers behind my back.

Even Mustaf is staring at me like I must be insane, but he hasn't moved so I keep going.

"Aha, you are caught **RED-HANDED**! Don't deny it, we know everything! We know exactly what you've been up to and what you have hidden in the boot of this limo!" I pause for effect (and to think of what to say next).

Mustaf's face goes blotchy and red. Milo ducks his head down and I put my hands up to protect myself, fearing the worst is about to happen.

But it doesn't.

To my surprise, Mustaf starts crying! Huge, scary, angry-looking Mustaf is actually weeping big fat tears. He obviously knows he's been caught out.

"Aha," I say triumphantly. "You know what you need to do to make it right, Mustaf."

"Neesh, look what you've done now! There, there, she didn't mean it," soothes Milo.

Glaring at Milo, I stand up to speak to Mustaf properly. "Is there something you need to tell us, Mustaf? I'm sure you'll feel much better if you come clean. Mum always says a problem shared is a problem halved. Come on – you can trust us. We can help."

Mustaf gulps loudly and reaches into his pocket with a gloved hand, pulling out the keys to the limo. He presses a button on the fob, the limo beeps and the boot clicks open behind us.

This is it – we are about to find Uncle Tony and **FINALLY** everything will be okay. I take a deep breath and look into the boot and see the napkin from earlier with some half-eaten food and next to that...a **BOX OF KITTENS**!

"I just couldn't leave them. I had to do something but I know I'm not supposed to keep personal belongings in the limousine. Your uncle would surely fire me if he finds out," Mustaf explains. "This is why I lose it with annoying neighbour man over there. I could not have him looking in the boot of the car and exposing me."

"So you haven't seen Uncle Tony today?" I ask, completely befuddled.

"No. I haven't seen your uncle since yesterday when I drove him and the twins home. Early this morning I received a message from **Mister Tony** on the mobile phone. It said I should collect **Master Manny** and **Miss Mindy** from near the theme park at 11.45 a.m. and bring them here. The message said he would be busy with wedding preparations until later. That was when I spotted this box of adorable defenceless kittens just left out on the road and I've been looking after them ever since. Even the twins do not know I had them in the boot."

Mustaf takes a deep breath and lifts the box of kittens from the boot. "Please, **I beg of you**, do not tell anyone about this. If I lose my job I cannot provide for them. They are my babies."

Milo nods in sympathy. "I understand, Mustaf, I would do the same." He leans in to the box and murmurs something to the kittens, then pauses, as if listening. "They say they really appreciate you saving them and can they please have some water?"

Mustaf smiles a weird, toothy smile – I don't think he does it very often. "Of course! Do you think you can help me, **young sir**?"

"I'd love to. Hey, I can introduce you to my lobster, he's just upstairs!" gasps Milo, and leads the big man into our house.

I scratch my head. Did all that really just happen? And there's something Mustaf said that is bugging me. My brain is tying itself in knots trying to figure it out. Maybe I'm overthinking it?

I start to follow Milo and Mustaf up to my

bedroom, but Mum comes racing down the stairs so fast I think she might take flight.

"Where's your dad, darling?" she trills. She is smiling with all her teeth, which looks a bit scary.

"In the kitchen. Are you okay, Mum?" I ask, raising my eyebrow at Granny, who is in the living room serving tea to a few of the remaining guests, probably as a cover for conducting her investigations.

Mum ignores me and flurries into the kitchen. Granny and I rush over and put our ears against the closed door.

"What do you mean, **MISSING**?" Dad asks.

"I mean **MISSING**. As in, not at home, not at work, not anywhere. Ricky just rang me on the mobile in a panic. He wanted to know if we'd seen him."

"Well, he must be somewhere; the wedding is tomorrow," Dad says.

"But what if he's run off? Got cold feet. You know, I always thought his aura was a bit off," Mum says.

"Oh, Bhagavan," Granny Jas swears. She peers at me over her spectacles and scratches her head. "Beta, it is looking like the news is out that your Uncle Tony is missing. Now whatever you do, **DON'T TELL BINDI**!"

CHAPTER 11

SECRET'S OUT!

"**DON'T TELL ME WHAT?!**" bellows Aunty Bindi, coming out of the downstairs bathroom. "It's the flowers, isn't it? I knew it! What's happened now?"

She looks like she's been through a washing machine, her hair sticking up in all directions, her arms and legs red from scrubbing the mehndi mess off. Aunty Suki emerges from the bathroom behind her, carrying what looks like the bucket and sponges that Dad uses to wash the car, sets them down by the kitchen door and disappears upstairs.

Mum and Dad burst out of the kitchen. "Everything okay?" they ask, even though they can clearly see it isn't and now they **BOTH** have huge, grinning, guilty smiles on their faces.

There are still quite a few guests in the living room and, like in a sci-fi movie when time freezes, everyone stops what they are doing and turns to see what's going on.

"**NO IT IS NOT!**" insists Aunty Bindi. "I just heard what Granny said and I want to know what's going on."

"Er...it's **nothing**," I say, waving frantically at Mum and Dad. But they're not looking at me. They're gawping at Bindi with a look of **pure panic**.

"Well, the thing is, you see, Ricky just phoned," Mum starts cautiously.

"And? What did he want, I'll ring him back now. Where's my phone?"

"Um, Aunty, I think you'd better sit down," I say, knowing there's no avoiding it now – we have to tell her the truth. Aunty Bindi looks at me then, worried because she knows I wouldn't normally speak up.

"What is it, Anni? Please **just tell me the truth** now," she says. "What did Ricky say?" Aunty Bindi is trembling. I don't know if it's because she's angry or cold or scared, but I've never seen her this way. I pull the grey fleecy blanket off the back of the sofa and put it round her shoulders. She grabs my hand and squeezes it.

"Well, Bindi, there's really no need to panic, I'm sure," Mum says slowly. "But it seems Tony hasn't turned up at his parents' house for the wedding preparations there today. They thought he might have snuck over here to see you, but I told them we haven't seen him. I mean, he could just be off having some quiet time before the big day? But he's not answering his phone and there doesn't seem to be any sign of him...anywhere."

Aunty Bindi starts crying but it's not her usual wailing. This is **REAL** sobbing, big fat tears rolling down her cheeks. "**THIS CAN'T BE**

HAPPENING!" she cries. "How could he do this to me?"

"What's going on?" Mindy and Manny come in slowly from the garden through the marquee.

"Oh, children, my dear sweetie pies! Come here! I have to tell you something." Bindi opens her arms to the twins but they don't move.

"Um, children, your dad's whereabouts are...well, that is to say...we don't quite know, exactly, or precisely, where he is," sputters Dad. "But he'll turn up, I'm sure," he says, regaining his best **Trust me, I'm a lawyer** voice.

"Why don't we all just sit down and try to stay calm?" Mum suggests. "I can bring through some of the gelebi."

"You mean you've lost our dad?" Manny says quietly to Bindi. "Well, I'm not surprised. Maybe he had second thoughts."

"That's a terrible thing to say!" Mindy elbows her brother. "I'm sure it's nothing to worry about.

He's probably just off organizing a surprise for you!"
She places her bag and notepad on the sideboard
and comes over to hold Bindi's hand, smiling a
sickly-sweet smile.

Aunty Bindi lets go of my now-throbbing hand
and lets Mindy comfort her.

"**Find Tony**," she mutters. "We must find him. I can't have a wedding with no groom. This is so humiliating!"

"**OH MY GOODNESS! IT'S A DISASTER!**" a voice yells from upstairs.

"Yes, yes, we know about Tony, no need for more dramatics." Granny Jas shakes her head. "These girls, always screaming and wailing. We didn't have that luxury in my day, you know!"

"No, I'm talking about this." Aunty Suki comes down the stairs holding a dripping wet mess of orange silk with a tear down the front and a broken strap. It takes me a second to realize it's my bridesmaid **lengha** top!

"I found it when I went to run a bath." Aunty Suki looks straight at me.

I look at Mum. Mum looks right back at me and she is not smiley or calm any more.

"Anni? What is this? Did you do this?"

"Mum, no, I would never. **It wasn't me**,"

I protest, standing up.

"You never liked that dress," Bindi sniffles. "You moaned enough about it when we chose it, so don't pretend you're sad about all this. Well, you've got your own way now."

"But I wouldn't destroy it! I couldn't." But I can see no one believes me. Dad shakes his head and walks away. Mum gives me her **too disappointed to scold** face and Bindi just turns her back on me. I can't believe this. I'm getting the blame for something I didn't do!

"But, Mum, Aunty Bindi, I think there might be someone else who wants to stop the wedding."

"I don't want to hear it right now, Anisha. I think you should go for a walk. We have too much to sort out here if this wedding is ever going to get back on track." Mum sighs and starts talking to Dad over Bindi's head about places they might look for Tony.

"Yes, Anisha, I think you've done enough damage, don't you?" Mindy calls out from the sofa as she strokes Bindi like she's a cat. There's something very weird about the way she's smiling and it makes my tummy lurch.

"C'mon, Neesh, let's get some fresh air." Milo appears at my side and guides me to the door. I can feel the guests staring at me as we leave. How has this happened? Everyone thinks it's my fault! We **HAVE** to find Tony and put this right.

As we leave we see a fire engine pulling up outside Mr Bogof's house. He spots us from where he is still hanging and starts pointing down at us and **SHOUTING**, so we duck behind the garden wall, and end up sitting on the steps in front of my house.

"It's not looking good. It's almost twenty-nine minutes past three – we're running out of time."

"Don't worry, Neesh, we can do this! Look, let's make a new list." Milo passes me a black spiral-bound notebook and a pen.

"Where did you get that notebook, Milo?" I ask slowly, realizing it looks very familiar.

"What? I just grabbed it off the sideboard in your house. I didn't think anyone would mind."

"Let me look at it for a second."

I open the notebook. Inside the pages are thick and creamy, with perforations down the side so you can tear them out easily. I've seen this paper somewhere before. I take the crumpled kidnapper's note out of my pocket and hand it to Milo.

"Look, Milo! It's the same kind of paper."

"That could have come from anywhere. You can't prove it's from this notebook."

I tear out a page from the notebook and look at it next to the kidnapper's note. Same thickness, same off-white colour. I hold the paper up and notice it has a watermark, a logo.

It's from Uncle Tony's mobile phone shop, Mega Mobiles! Yes, Uncle Tony's car has a sticker in the back window with the same symbol on it.

"Check the note, Milo. Does it have this watermark on it?"

Milo holds the note up to the light and I see it straight away – the same watermark is on both the notepad paper and the kidnapper's note.

Suddenly **I feel very sick**. My stomach churns like when I accidentally ended up on the Deathspin ride at the fairground that time. I thought I was queuing for the weird-science tent and by the time I realized the truth, it was too late – I was being flung around at the speed of light! (Okay, maybe not the actual speed of light, but close enough.)

"Neesh, what is it? Are you okay?"

"Milo, it all makes sense now. It's so obvious, how did we miss it?"

"Miss what?"

"**THE TWINS!** It's them – they're the ones!"

"They can't be – you said they couldn't have done it. The note arrived before they got here."

"Yes, but think about it. I'm pretty sure that's Mindy's notepad – you said you got it off the sideboard and that's where Mindy put her stuff when she came in from the garden."

"Okay, but why would they kidnap their own dad and want to stop the wedding?"

"Because of their mum. You heard Uncle Ricky, he said it earlier. They get upset about their mum being in **Bollywood** and they're **not happy** about their dad remarrying. It's definitely them, Milo – I don't know exactly how they did it but the notepaper is **proof**. I need to speak to my mum – she'll have to listen to me now!"

Mum is on her phone when I go into the living room. Most of the guests seem to have been scared off by Bindi's sobbing earlier, so the house is much quieter. Aunty Suki is trying to clean up the marquee and Aunty Bindi must be upstairs.

The twins are nowhere to be seen. I hover round Mum, trying to get her attention, but she turns away from me.

"Yes, terrible, isn't it! Well, of course we have no idea where he is. I keep suggesting we call the police, but Bindi won't hear of it," Mum tells whoever is on the other end of the phone.

I wave my hands desperately in front of her.

"Anni, will you stop!" Mum shoos me away.

"But I need to tell you SOMETHING! Something important about Uncle Tony!" I yell.

Mum covers the mouthpiece to the phone and says, "I'm listening, what is it?"

"I know who's behind all this, Mum. It's **THE TWINS**!"

"What? What do you mean?" said Mum.

"It's the twins! They've **kidnapped** Uncle Tony!" I say.

"What? Don't be ridiculous! Why and how would they even do such a terrible thing? It's

PREPOSTEROUS! They're such sweet kids! I can't believe that."

"No, but, Mum, you don't understand! I have proof! Well, sort of proof – there was a note but I didn't tell you about it before because I thought I could sort it all out. And I'm not sure how they did it, but I wouldn't put anything past those two. Maybe they hit him over the head with one of Granny's prize mangoes..."

Mum rubs the side of her head. "Anni, what are you talking about? This is **NONSENSE**. First you wreck your bridesmaid's dress, now you're trying to blame the twins. There's a lot to do and I have to try and calm your aunty down. She's insisting on going ahead with the wedding tomorrow – she's convinced Tony is going to turn up. We just have to hope that he does! Run along, please, and no more of this talk, okay?" And with that Mum turns her back on me again and carries on chatting on the phone.

I walk out to Milo, who's still sitting on the steps

in front of my house. "How'd it go?" he says, looking up hopefully.

"No one believes me. It's no good. They've won. We might as well **GIVE UP**!"

CHAPTER 12

NO ONE MESSES WITH MY AUNTY!

Just as I'm sitting there, slumped on the steps in defeat, a voice above my head says, "Now **what is all this about giving up**? Have I taught you nothing? How many times do I say it? It's not over till it's over." I look up to see Granny Jas poking her head out of the living room window at the front of the house.

"Oh...hi, Granny."

"So, why are you talking **NONSENSE** about giving up, hmm?" Granny asks again in a stern voice.

I look at Milo and Milo looks at me. I take a deep

breath and tell Granny Jas what we've discovered about the **EVIL TWINS**.

"...And I tried to explain it to Mum but now she thinks that I don't want the wedding to go ahead. I know I wasn't, like, over the moon about wearing that hideous dress, but I would never destroy it, Granny! You have to believe me!"

Granny listens carefully and strokes the little hairs on her chin. "Well, well, well, they are **little monkeys**, aren't they? We will have to do something about this," she says.

"You believe me?" I say. Suddenly I feel lighter.

"Of course, beta! I know you have a good heart and you wouldn't tell lies to Granny. We must be dealing with these two naughty twins."

"But how?" I say, frustrated. "We have no idea where Uncle Tony could be and the wedding is tomorrow! It's already forty-one minutes past three!"

"Ha, yes! I know, my darling. But you have

something much more powerful than those mischievous twins."

"She does?" Milo looks puzzled.

"I do?" I'm puzzled too.

Granny Jas chuckles. "Yes, silly! **You are the only calm one in the family!** The rest of us go completely crazy when there is a crisis but you, **beta**, you see things, you think carefully – you are the only one in the house putting two and two together and not coming up with fifty-five!"

"Do you really think I can handle it?" I ask her. "I'm not sure I can outsmart them. They've had me running round in circles all day!"

"So, we should just give up then? No point in even trying if they're that clever?" Granny Jas is now leaning dangerously out of the window. Her sari blows in the wind like a parachute as she shakes her head. "You just stay there and give me one minute, beta." And she disappears inside the house.

"We can't give up, Neesh!" insists Milo. "You

can't let them win. Just imagine how sad Aunty Bindi will be!"

I think about Aunty Bindi – crazy, annoying Aunty Bindi, with her screeching and wailing. Desperately upset Aunty Bindi squeezing my hand, asking us to find Uncle Tony as she sobbed on the sofa. I have to do something. She might be my annoying aunty, but she is **MY AUNTY** and no one messes with the people I love.

I stand up, determined. "I'll do it," I say, stamping my foot.

I'm going to have to sort this mess out. First things first, we have to find Tony. The twins must have made a mistake somewhere along the way and we have to find it.

"**Beta!**" Granny Jas reappears at the window just as we're about to walk away. "You might need this." She tosses something through the air. It's hard and hits me right on **the head**. It's not until I look down and pick it up that I realize it is Manny's tablet with the skateboarding cover.

"Granny, how did you get hold of this?" I shriek. Luckily, it's still in one piece after the fall.

"Well, you see now, Granny Jas is still useful to you kids. I can be a pocket-pick when I need to." She chuckles. "Plus, that Manny is in the toilet and Mindy is too busy watching vampire programmes with her daft dog to notice what I was getting up to."

Finally, something that might be able to help us find Uncle Tony – and we'd better do it fast!

CHAPTER 13

A CLUE!

"Quick, Milo, let's see what's on Manny's tablet,"
I say, pushing the ON button.

We watch in anticipation as the tablet comes
to life. The password screen comes up and my heart
sinks.

"Oh no! Now what?" Milo scratches his head.

"C'mon, let's think. What could it be? Something
that means a lot to Manny."

"Hair gel?" Milo jokes.

I try it because, well, you never know. It doesn't
work.

A message flashes up on the screen: This device
will lock after three failed login attempts.

"Okay, we have to be smart about this. What do we know about Mindy and Manny, apart from them being mean?" I say, more to myself than anything.

"Well, Manny likes football, doesn't he? Maybe it's his favourite team!" Milo suggests.

"No, he **pretends** to like football because Uncle Tony likes it. I've seen him watching skateboarding, that's much more his thing."

"What about his favourite music? Wasn't he wearing a T-shirt with that band on it? Oh, wait, what are they called?"

"**Black Lightning**, I think. I guess it's worth a try." And I type it in.

The screen flashes up: Incorrect password. You have one more attempt before this tablet is locked.

Oh no, we can't mess this up. My tummy does a funny turn again – we have to get this right. Uncle Tony and the wedding depend on it.

"What about Mindy? She's all goth and into **vampires**. Maybe it's something to do with that?" Milo suggests.

"No, it's Manny's tablet. It must be something to do with him…or…" And just like that I've got it. "Both of them!"

"Both of them?"

I smile. "Yes, Milo. What or who connects them both – someone who means a lot to them…?"

Milo looks at me like I'm speaking in another language.

"Their mum!" I yell. "It's their mum's name, I just know it!"

"Their mum? Isn't she in India? Do you even know her name?"

"Yes, because Bindi idolizes her, even though she's Uncle Tony's first wife, which is a bit weird. But Aunty Bindi loves Bollywood and the twins' mum is in a load of Bollywood movies. Bindi even made me watch one with her recently, it was cringe!

But I remember now, the twins' mum is called Biyanka Bachan."

"So, type it in. That must be it!"

I tap the keys, my heart thumping in my throat. B-I-Y-A-N-K-A.

And it works! We're in!

"Check the internet search history. There might be clues in there," Milo urges.

"What, like, how to kidnap your dad in ten easy steps?" I roll my eyes but click onto the tab that shows us all the websites Manny last visited anyway.

How to be cool in ten short lessons.

(Wow. Just, wow.)

Trendy hairstyles for boys.

(Oh dear.)

Plot your way to becoming a super-villain.

(This is a bit worrying. Maybe I'd better

show Uncle Tony this one when we find him.)

Five signs your stepmother is an alien.
(Really?)

The Birmingham South-West Aspire Junior Middle High Academy School website.
(That's our school – it used to just be Aspire Juniors but every year the title gets longer! More importantly, the twins don't even go there.)

"That's a bit weird. Why would they be looking at our school website?" Milo asks.

"I don't know but it could be a **clue**. Seems a bit suspicious that of all the schools they could be looking at, they'd choose ours."

I click the link to the school website page they were looking at and the ABOUT US page comes up with a gallery of staff photographs: the caretaker, Mr Bristles, looking grumpy; our teacher Mr Helix in a cheesy group photo with the other class teachers; then a picture of our PE teacher, Miss Bench, holding a cricket bat. There's one of our school librarian, Mr Bound, standing proudly in front of the library, and then finally the head teacher, Mr Graft, looking stern as usual.

"Do you think we should check it out, Neesh? It could be important, it just seems too weird not to be **a clue**. We could be there by four o' clock – school is only ten minutes away if we run. The school gates stay open till five because of the gymnastics club and the dance academy that run on Saturdays."

"How do you know that, Milo?"

"I...er...may have tried out for gymnastics once." Milo blushes. "I thought it might be fun. You have to be really strong to do it, you know."

I shake my head with a smile. "Milo, you are full of surprises! You're right, we should check it out.

Come on, there's no time to lose!" I say, jumping up.
"Let me just tell Granny where we're going."

We run all the way to the school, so we're really
out of breath by the time we get there. Granny Jas
has given us her phone to call home if we need to.
I clutch it tightly. Our school is not that far from my
house and sometimes I walk part of the way just with
Milo if Mum leaves me at the corner when she's on
her way to her meditation class. But still, I kind of
wish Mum or Dad or even Aunty Bindi were here
with us. It feels like a big deal, going off by ourselves
to try to find clues. I mean, there might not even **BE**
any clues. I shake that thought off. Time is running
out, we have to at least **TRY** every possibility. That's
what a good scientist or detective would do.

The playground is busy with parents waiting for
children to finish gymnastics and dance, and little
kids running round chasing one another. No one
asks us why we're there, so we make our way to the
main building without stopping. We walk in through

151

the main doors and the sound of music and feet thumping on the school-hall floor fills the empty corridor. To the left of us the doors to the hall suddenly fling open and Mr Notes the music teacher marches out into the corridor, looking left and right before his beady eyes land on us.

"Ah, there you are."

Milo and I look at each other, confused.

"Er, sorry, sir, we have to get goi—"

"No time to dilly-dally! Come along, we need to do another run-through before the end of the lesson."

I look around. We'll just have to go along with it and escape at the first chance we get.

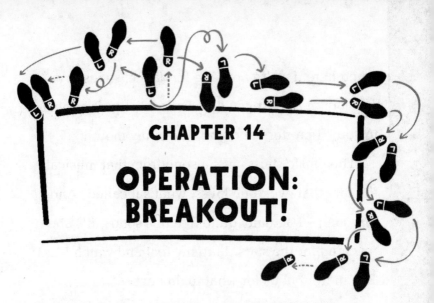

CHAPTER 14

OPERATION: BREAKOUT!

Milo and I shuffle into the hall behind Mr Notes.

In front of us, ten kids stand on the stage in a line.

The dance teacher, Miss Jive, is in front of them.

"Here they are, Miss Jive," Mr Notes says as he

sits down at the piano.

Miss Jive beckons us forward. "Ah, okay, come

on, you two, into the line please, quickly quickly, no

time to waste." She nods at Mr Notes. "And **a five,**

six...a five, six, seven, EIGHT!"

"What do we do?" Milo panics. "We don't do

dance!"

"I know, but we don't have a good reason for

being here if we're not here for dance, so just try and join in as best you can. Follow the person next to you," I mutter out of the side of my mouth.

The music starts – it's a song from that musical, the film that everyone loves, what's it called? And this song – I actually quite like this song – it's about reaching for the stars. I tap my foot and watch Miss Jive in front of us for what to do next.

First she takes a step to the left, then one to the right. Okay, that was easy enough. Then a step back with the left foot and a step to the right with the other foot. I accidentally step on Milo but manage to correct myself. Then it's a hand reaching up and a hand on my hip and – oops – I hit the girl on the other side of me. I try to mouth the word **SORRY**, but she just glares at me and keeps dancing. Milo, on the other hand, is doing quite well when I look over – he seems to have more rhythm than me. I think he's enjoying himself; he even throws in a little hip-wiggle! Unfortunately, his wiggle is quite wide and a bit too enthusiastic and sends the person to his right tumbling into the next person, setting off a domino effect, until pretty much the whole of that side of the line is scrambling in a heap on the floor.

Just then two kids from the year below us walk into the hall and stare at us, totally freaked out. I didn't think we were that bad!

"Ah, you two, where have you been? **I thought you two were those two!**" Mr Notes points at Milo and me in exasperation. "Did you find the caretaker to sort that leak backstage?" he asks them.

"No, sir, we went to his office. There were some weird noises coming out of there but it was locked and there's no sign of Mr Bristles anywhere," the boy answers.

"I reckon that room's **HAUNTED**," mutters the girl.

"Right, well, okay, let's get on, shall we? I'll find Mr Bristles later." Mr Notes waves them away and looks back at his sheet music.

Milo and I look at each other. "**Weird noises!**" we whisper.

"Um, may we be excused now, Miss Jive?" I ask.

"Yes, off you go, I think we've seen quite enough from you two, run along! Right, class, pick yourselves up, no time for lying down, let's try again, shall we?" And the music starts up again, along with a thundering of feet stomping the stage.

When we get outside into the corridor I say to Milo, "We need a key for the caretaker's office. I bet the head teacher has keys to all the rooms in the school. Let's go and see if they're in his office. He won't be around today."

The door to Mr Graft's office creaks loudly as I push it open. Milo grabs my arm and follows me in.

I've never been in here before – you only get sent to the head teacher if you've done something **REALLY** bad. A shiver runs up my spine. Is it cold in here? I don't do stuff like this, I follow the rules. That statue on the shelf of some weird old man's head is judging me, I just know it!

"Check all the drawers in this desk, Milo," I say, as I search the cabinet behind it.

"Ooh, look!" I hear a moment later. "It's all the stuff Mr Graft has confiscated off kids this term.

He keeps it till the last day, you know. I think that's quite harsh. **Wow, my light-up yo-yo!**"

"Milo, put it back! We could get in real trouble if anyone realizes we've been in here."

"Oh, okay, I suppose."

"Look, I've found the master key! Come on, this should open the caretaker's office – **LET'S GO**!"

I peek around the head teacher's door into the corridor before we creep out. The school is still bustling with classes finishing up. We'd better be quick before someone sees us. I check the time on Granny's phone. It is eleven minutes past four.

We run down the hallway and around the corner to the caretaker's office.

"**QUICK**, Milo, hold the phone while I unlock the door."

"This is it, Neesh. Your uncle is behind that door, it's all going to be okay – **you've saved the wedding**!" Milo smiles.

I take a deep breath and turn the key in the lock,

press down on the handle and open the door to find—

"You're not Uncle Tony!" I yell.

"Mr Bristles?" Milo gawks at our school caretaker, who appears to be pointing a mop at us and wearing a bucket on his foot.

I gulp, then pull myself together. "It's okay, Mr Bristles, we're here to help. We thought you were someone else."

"Oh, **thank my lucky mops** you came along!" he gasps.

"Milo, quick! Get Mr Bristles a cup of water from the cooler in the corridor.

"What happened, Mr Bristles?" I ask him as Milo's trainers squeak away down the hallway.

159

I help Mr Bristles remove the bucket from his foot while he talks.

"I don't really know. I was putting away my broom this morning and suddenly someone pushed me in from behind and locked the door. I tried **shouting** for help but those dance classes are so **LOUD** no one heard me! It was so blinking dark in 'ere with the door shut that while I was trying to find the light switch I stepped in that bucket and then I couldn't get it off. When I heard the key turning in the lock just now I didn't know who it was so I got ready with the nearest thing I could find – that mop!"

I blink hard. I can't believe it! I sigh, putting my head in my hands. "We've wasted all this time and we **still** haven't found Uncle Tony! It's too late. The wedding won't be able to go ahead now. **WE'VE FAILED!**"

Just at that moment Milo comes back in and hands the caretaker a cup of water.

"Well, I don't know about no wedding, but I've missed getting to work because of this mucking about," Mr Bristles groans.

"Er...Mr Bristles, you are **AT** work," I point out.

"I mean my other work, at the theme park. Caretaking don't pay much, you know. I moonlight as the vampire in a coffin down the road at the Creaky Towers theme park. I usually open up here on a Saturday morning, do any odd jobs, and then head over there for a few hours in the afternoon. It's alright, as jobs go. But they'll probably fire me now, seeing as I didn't turn up today for work." He grunts unhappily.

I notice Milo nodding. "Did you know about this?" I ask.

"Obviously, everyone knows Mr B is the vampire at Creaky Towers, he's **awesome**! There was a piece in the local paper about him and everything – **caretaker by day, vampire undertaker by night**!" Milo chuckles.

Mr Bristles, 59, on the graveyard shift.

"I'll have to phone my boss," Mr Bristles grumbles. "They'll never believe I was locked in my own office though. Thanks for getting me out of there, kids, but I really best be on my way." And with that, he hobbles off.

We head back to the house in silence, with **despair** hanging over us, **BLACK** and **GLOOMY**. Even Milo can't find anything hopeful to say. It feels like everything we've done has been for nothing.

As we walk, the events of the day whirl round in my head: the note, the phone call, Uncle Ricky, Granny Jas, Mustaf and now Mr Bristles. All the things we've discovered and we're still no closer to finding Uncle Tony. No one except Milo and Granny Jas will believe that the twins are involved, especially because they have the alibi of being at the theme park this morning.

The theme park...

THE THEME PARK!

Oh no...**CREAKY TOWERS** is all spooky-themed – I do not like being spooked **AT ALL**.

Reluctantly, I turn to Milo. "Where did Mustaf say he picked the twins up from?"

"The theme park," Milo replies.

"And where does Mr Bristles work as a second job?"

"**The...theme...park,**" Milo answers cautiously.

"So that's where we need to investigate. I'm sure of it! Come on, we need to talk to Mustaf!" And with that, we run the rest of the way home.

When we get there, Mustaf is outside polishing the car. He looks up just as we approach.

"Ah, children, I would not venture inside if I were you. Your aunt is, shall we say, a bit upset." Mustaf grimaces, his moustache turning down. I can hear the **WAILING** wafting out through the living-room window. I grimace too.

"We need to ask you something, Mustaf. It's really important, and it could put all this right and get Uncle Tony home in time for the wedding."

Mustaf places the polishing cloth on the bonnet of the car and stands up straight, towering over us. "Ask me anything! Your uncle has been very good to me over the years, so please, how can I help?"

"Well, we think the twins are behind all this but we can't prove it yet. Can you think of anything

164

suspicious they might have said or done while you've been driving them around today."

Mustaf twirls the end of his moustache for a moment. "Well, not really. Actually it was yesterday when I picked them up."

"Yesterday!" I knew there was something bugging me earlier when we talked to Mustaf. That's it. The twins didn't come home this morning like I've been assuming all this time. They came home yesterday!

Mustaf goes on, "They were supposed to be coming home today but actually Mister Tony called me and said that the twins wanted to have some quality time with him before the wedding and so they were coming home early. So yesterday I picked them up and drove them straight home. Oh, wait, no, we did make a brief stop. At that hardware store on Griffiths Drive. Something about getting stuff for a homework project. Today I picked them up from the theme park as instructed and brought them here.

Their dad had taken them there but the message I got said he had gone to do some jobs in preparation for the wedding. Now I think about it, the twins asked me to make a stop today too. On the way back from the theme park they asked me to stop at your school actually, which did seem a little strange but I didn't query it. They are often quite demanding. Anyway, they went in for about ten minutes and came out looking very pleased with themselves. It is not the usual way for me to ask questions, I had no reason to think anything of it. I am sorry."

"Don't worry, Mustaf, you've been really helpful. Could I look in the back of the limo where the twins were sitting?"

"Of course, miss, help yourself." Mustaf opens the passenger door of the limo for me and stands to the side. I crawl in and the smell of fresh leather fills my nostrils. The car is spotless, apart from a piece of crumpled paper poking out from under the floor mat. I lean over and grab it. **A RECEIPT!** So that's what

they bought from the hardware shop: a **padlock**!
It's all coming together.

"What did you find?" Milo asks as I clamber out
in a not-very-ladylike manner.

"**PROOF!**" I say triumphantly, waving the
receipt. "Mustaf, can you drive us somewhere?
It's really URGENT."

"Yes, miss. May I be so bold as to ask where we
are going?" Mustaf ushers us into the limo and gets
into the driver's seat.

Milo and I fasten our seatbelts. "**To the theme
park, CREAKY TOWERS!**"

CHAPTER 15

THINGS THAT GO BUMP...

As Mustaf drives, Milo turns to me in the back of the limo and asks, "What's going on, Neesh? What proof did you find and why are we going to the theme park? I don't think now is the time for an afternoon out."

"It's starting to make sense, Milo. Mustaf told us that the twins got him to take them to a hardware shop on the way home yesterday. I'd forgotten till now because I was so busy trying to get away from him, but my cousin Akshay mentioned he'd seen them in the shop yesterday too. Anyway, do you know what they bought? **A padlock!**"

"Okay..." Milo still looks confused.

"A **padlock**, Milo! Think about it. Why would they need a **padlock**?"

"Um, maybe to lock up a bike?"

"No, Milo! Don't you see? Maybe they used the padlock to lock up Uncle Tony somewhere in the theme park!"

"Oh, right, I get it!" Milo exclaims, but he still looks confused.

"I think I know how it all happened, Milo," I continue. "So imagine: the twins convince their dad to let them come home a night earlier than planned and not to tell anyone so they can just have time together, the three of them. Then this morning the twins ask their dad to take them to the theme park for their last bit of time with him before the wedding. Uncle Tony **LOVES** theme parks! So they set off early to make the most of the day. Somehow the twins **lock him up somewhere** and then, using his phone, they text Mustaf to come and collect them."

Milo raises his eyebrow at me but says nothing.

I can tell by his face that he thinks I've really lost it now. I keep going. I know I'm babbling but I have to get it out.

"Then they get Mustaf to take them to our school, and they shove Mr Bristles into the office."

"But why, Neesh? What does Mr Bristles have to do with it all?"

"I'm not sure, but it's all connected, I just know it."

Just then we see the sign for Creaky Towers and the limo turns into a gravel driveway. My stomach turns – I hate creepy stuff.

Fear of dark spooky places
+
Creaky Towers theme park
+
stir in a chill in the air
+
some ghoulish goings on
=
Goosebumps for me!

It's **sixteen minutes and fourteen seconds past five now** and the theme park shuts in **forty-four minutes**. We have to find Uncle Tony – and **FAST**.

At the ticket entrance, Mustaf stops to pay for us, while Milo and I race ahead, grabbing a map from a woman wearing a **CREAKY TOWERS** sandwich board on the way. The park is busy and all I can see are grown-ups and kids criss-crossing in front of me, trying to get on their last few rides before the park closes. Milo and I look at each other, panicked. Where do we even start?

Mustaf catches us up and the three of us stand there in the middle of the park, looking around at all the different rides. There are so many! **MUMMY'S REVENGE** – a roller coaster that takes you down into the mouth of a mummy. **THE HENCHMAN'S HAMMER**, which swings violently from side to side. **THE SPINNING PHANTOMS**, which is like a teacups ride but spooky and a lot faster. I feel ill watching the people on the rides being flung about, side to side, round and round, up and down.

"I'm sure there must be a connection with Mr Bristles – maybe we should start with the ride he works on. Milo! He said he works as a vampire. Where can we find vampires and coffins here?" I ask, narrowly dodging a zombie selling ice cream.

"What about there?" Mustaf points to the Haunted House. The sign in front of it says

BEWARE OF THE BATS!

"Do you think they mean real bats? Hey, maybe they'll know something! I could ask – I think I know a few words in batish," Milo exclaims happily.

A smile creeps up my face and I realize I'm so glad Milo is here with me.

"It's worth a try," I say. "While you're checking it out, I'll go and see if I can find someone to help us."

There's no queue so Mustaf and Milo go straight into the **HAUNTED HOUSE**. I look around for an information point or a member of staff. I pull out the map and try to figure out where we are.

"**BOO!**" A kid with a monster mask makes me jump.

"That's not funny!" I yell after him as he runs off laughing.

"Can you help me a second? I'm looking for—" I try to ask a zombie, but he only **grunts** and **groans** at me. This is hopeless!

Just then Milo comes flying out of the **HAUNTED HOUSE** closely followed by Mustaf.

"Sorry, we didn't mean to disturb you!" Milo calls over his shoulder.

"What happened?" I ask, as Mustaf brushes cobwebs off his shoulders.

"Um, I'll tell you later. Let's just say the bats were not feeling very talkative!" Milo admits.

I look again at the time and it's already **twenty-three minutes past five**. Time seems to be speeding up, even though I know that's scientifically impossible.

"It's useless. We're never going to find Uncle Tony," I whisper.

"Don't give up yet, Neesh." Milo puts his hand on my shoulder. "You can do this, we've come this far. Just stay calm and think. We're looking for a ride with vampires, where someone could be trapped and not found for ages."

I realize he's right. There can't be **THAT** many places where you could trap someone without them being discovered pretty quickly. And so I guess we only need to look for vampire rides.

A voice over the tannoy interrupts my thoughts: "ALL RIDES WILL CLOSE IN TWENTY MINUTES. ALL ABOARD THE LAST RIDES OF THE DAY. THANK YOU FOR VISITING CREAKY TOWERS. MWAH HAHAHA!"

I start to panic again – it's so hard to see anything over the crowds and this map is useless. I look up at Mustaf in despair, and suddenly I have an idea!

"Mustaf, can you lift Milo onto your shoulders? Milo, look for vampire rides!"

Mustaf leans down and Milo climbs up. "**Wow**, I can see the whole park from up here!" he marvels. "Did you know they have a zoo here as well? We have to go and see the lions!"

"Milo, focus – can you see any vampire rides?"

"Um, wait…yes **DRACULA'S DEN**! That must be it!" Milo yelps.

"Quick, which way, Milo?"

"This way – let's go, Mustaf!"

We weave through the crowds, me running behind Mustaf with Milo on his shoulders, who's pointing which way to go. Most people are walking in the opposite direction, towards the exits. "Watch where you're going!" a person dressed in a ghostly sheet shouts out, but we keep running, dodging elbows and bags. People really get dressed up to come here, don't they!

Suddenly it's in front of us. I look up and up and up some more. **DRACULA'S DEN** looms over us, dark and terrifying. This has got to be it.

"In there?" Milo murmurs. "**COOL!**"

I stare at Milo. "Really? Aren't you scared?"

"Nope, it looks **awesome**! C'mon, let's go!"

"Er...I don't think I can." My feet are rooted to the ground, refusing to move.

"You have to! We need to find your uncle. C'mon! You've been so brave through all this. Don't give up now!"

I sigh. He's right. I **HAVE** to do this. Milo gets down from Mustaf's shoulders and they walk up to the

entrance. I reluctantly follow. There's no queue and the attendant looks like he's about to close up.

"Excuse me, is there a vampire in a coffin on this ride?" I ask lamely.

The attendant points up at the sign and smirks. "Well, yeah, it's **DRACULA'S DEN**. Duh. But I'm just closing up, sorry, dudes." The attendant shrugs and goes to pull a rope across the entrance. But then Mustaf steps forward. The ride attendant looks up, mouth hanging open.

"Er, I mean, if you really want to go on it that badly, yeah, of course, hop in. The vampire in the coffin is near the end of the ride, but he **didn't turn up** this afternoon anyway." And with that he runs into his little cubicle where the ride controls are.

Mustaf rubs his beard. "What was his problem? I only wanted to ask him where we pay for the car parking."

"No time to worry about that, let's get on this ride. We have to find that coffin."

I step into the rickety wooden carriage, which doesn't feel very safe. I sit down, feeling grateful for Milo piling in next to me. We pull the belt across our laps. I wonder if anyone's done a risk assessment round here recently. Before I can ask, the ride rattles to life and starts moving into **DRACULA'S DEN**.

Inside it's **dark and gloomy** as the carriage shakes slowly down the tracks; shadows dance about on the walls of the tunnel and the only light comes from a few dim lamps. There's a cold breeze coming from somewhere. I cross my arms around myself and shiver while Milo grins happily. I peer over the side to make sure there's nothing about to jump out at me. Above us, cobwebs hang down from the ceiling and I'm sure I feel a spider crawling down my neck. **Howling noises** and **ghoulish sounds** bounce around us as we move through the tunnel.

Milo makes whistling noises and shouts, "Cool!" and "No way!" when things jump out at us. "Aren't you having fun, Neesh?" he asks. He's enjoying this **way** too much. Mustaf is totally silent in the carriage in front of us, which is even more spooky.

Suddenly a plastic skeleton **boings** out from the wall and brushes against my hair.

I scream: "**AAARGH!**"

I can't do this. Why did I think I could? Then I think of Granny urging me on. "**Come on, beta, you can do it, almost there now. You're not going to let some silly old vampires beat you, are you?**"

I straighten up
and say to Milo,
"The attendant said the coffin is near
the end of the ride. Keep a lookout."

We rattle on along the track. There's an
echo in the tunnel and more weird **ghoulish** sounds.
It's even darker here, but I keep looking, determined
to find Uncle Tony. We're close, I can feel it.

"Look! It's right up ahead – we'll have to jump
out," Milo shouts gleefully.

I never knew he liked being scared so much! I look to where he's pointing and I see it. The coffin is propped up against the wall near the end of the tunnel. It's black and has a silver vampire-bat sign on the top.

I undo my belt and hop out of the carriage. Luckily it's a slow ride. Mustaf and Milo do the same. We stand to the side as the rest of the carriages rattle past us and then run over to the coffin. Then I hear it – a thumping coming from inside. It's faint but there's **DEFINITELY SOMEONE IN THERE!**

RIP

I TOLD YOU I WAS SICK

CHAPTER 16

THE GHOULISH GROOM

The coffin is firmly shut and a padlock – which must be the one the twins bought from the hardware shop – is securing the latch, so there's no way to open the coffin without force. I notice a few air holes in the top of the coffin. Mr Bristles or the theme park staff must have put them in for when he's doing his vampire bit.

"Uncle Tony? Is that you in there?" I feel I'd better check. I have got it wrong a few times today.

"Yes, thank goodness! **PLEASE, PLEASE GET ME OUT OF HERE!**" comes the muffled reply.

It **IS** Uncle Tony! I look up at Mustaf. "Do you think you can get it open?"

Mustaf smiles then and cracks his knuckles, which makes me scrunch up my face. He places one big hand either side of the coffin and pulls. The coffin creaks in protest, but doesn't give way. For a second I think we might have to just lift the whole coffin out of there and figure out how to open it later.

"**DON'T WORRY, UNCLE TONY, WE'LL GET YOU OUT!**" I yell hopefully.

Mustaf takes a deep breath and pulls this weird face like he's trying to **POO**. He tugs the lid with all his strength and suddenly it pops off like the top of a jam jar. We all jump back in surprise and see a very sweaty-looking Uncle Tony rubbing his eyes and looking around.

Milo cheers and does a little **victory dance**, Mustaf dusts himself off, and I...well, I forget about being calm and avoiding drama and I launch myself at Uncle Tony, almost knocking him sideways. I've never been so glad to see anyone, ever.

"Steady on, Anni," Uncle Tony chuckles. "We're not even properly related yet. Have I missed the wedding? Please say I haven't. **Is Bindi okay?**"

"No, Uncle, don't worry, you haven't missed it. We've been looking for you everywhere! We thought Uncle Ricky had kidnapped you and then we – well, mostly me – thought Granny Jas was behind it, and then we finally figured out it was the twins!" I babble – and then I realize Uncle Tony is sobbing.

"I was so happy when they suggested a day out at the theme park, just the three of us. I have been so worried they wouldn't accept my marriage to Bindi but, you know, I thought they wanted me to be **happy**."

Milo pats Uncle Tony on the shoulder sympathetically. "I don't understand how they got you in the coffin in the first place."

"They said this was their favourite ride. They told me the vampire jumping out of the coffin was the best bit, but the attendant at the entrance told us there would be no vampire as he only works evenings and weekends. The twins were so disappointed, so as we went round on the track they asked me to pretend to be him, just for a laugh. I was so eager to please them I jumped into the coffin and I didn't realize it was a trick until Mindy threw in some **chocolate** and **bottled water** before they locked me in there. I suppose I should be thankful they thought of that." Uncle Tony rubs his eyes some more. "I'm extremely grateful that you all came to find me. Really, words cannot express." Uncle Tony looks at all three of us then with tears in his eyes. Mustaf seems to have something in his eye too, and turns away.

"I'm sorry we didn't get here sooner, Uncle Tony, but we're here now and Aunty Bindi will be so glad to have you back."

"My **SWEETUMS**! Is she okay? I must see her! Oh, but it's bad luck to see the bride before the big day, isn't it?"

"I think you've already had all the bad luck!" Milo mumbles.

"Look, we can phone Aunty Bindi and let her know you're okay – I have Granny's phone," I say.

"Oh, thank you, Anni! Thank you for not giving up – you know, you are **really amazing**." Uncle shakes his head, smiling while he dials Aunty Bindi's mobile number.

They have a really **mushy lovey-dovey** conversation with lots of cooing and blowing kisses down the phone. Meanwhile Milo runs to tell the ride attendant what's happened and that we're coming out and not to shut everything down yet. The attendant insists on radioing the park manager, a rather flustered little man who appears after a few minutes, quite out of breath and pink in the cheeks.

"I don't know how this could have happened, I'm so very sorry, sir. Please accept our sincere apologies and these annual passes for you and your family!"

"I don't think we'll be coming back anytime soon," I mutter, but Uncle Tony smiles at the man and tells him not to worry and thank you for the gesture. He's much more chilled out about everything than I would be!

I glance at my watch. It's **three minutes after six o' clock**.

"Quick, Uncle Tony, let's get out of here before we're all locked in the theme park overnight. Aunty Bindi definitely won't be fine if that happens! We need to get you home – **tomorrow is the big day**!"

CHAPTER 17

A BIG FAT FABULOUS WEDDING

The next morning, the morning of the wedding, I am dressed and ready to go before everyone else. Surprisingly, the orange bridesmaid lengha actually looks okay. Aunty Suki managed to dry it out and stitch up the tear. Mum found a silk scarf to drape over my shoulder that covers up the mended bit. I mean, I wouldn't wear it every day but it could be worse.

Mum said the twins finally owned up to being the ones who wrecked it. They said it was accidental, but I know it wasn't. No one believes them after everything that's happened anyway. Dad said we should let Uncle Tony deal with them and that the main thing is that everyone is safe and well. I did see Granny Jas waggling her finger at them in the marquee, but then the most surprising thing happened – she **HUGGED** them! Manny hugged her back too. I think he might not be so bad, deep **DEEP** down. Mindy just stood there, looking a bit startled. I don't think she knew what to do.

As I sit in our living room this morning I listen to the stomping around upstairs and Aunty Bindi singing happily as she gets ready. I think back to the conversation I overheard last night from outside the kitchen, before Mustaf took the twins back to Uncle Tony's.

"I can't believe the wedding is going ahead." That was Mindy. "I thought we'd stopped it for sure. It's all Anisha's fault. Now Dad is going to marry that horrid woman and our mum will never come back."

"I know, but there's nothing we can do now," Manny had replied. "Plus I'm not sure she **is** that horrid. You know, on the first day of term before we went back to boarding school she ironed my shirt and helped me do my tie. It was nice having someone to care about me like a mum does."

"**She's not our mum, Manny**, don't forget that," Mindy warned him. "Dad can iron your shirts or, better still, learn to do it yourself!"

"I guess." Manny didn't sound that certain. "But, sis, our mum's not here. She doesn't even email or call."

"Well, she must be busy. She is a **Bollywood star**, Manny. Try and understand," Mindy scolded him. "Plus, who says Bindi is going to be so great?

People like that are always nice in the beginning. You should know that. She'll just be putting on an act for Dad. It's not real – she probably just wants his money."

"I think you're wrong, Mindy. I think we have to at least give her a chance. She seems to make Dad happy and maybe it would be okay to be part of Anisha's family. Look how nice they are to us, even after everything we did!"

Mindy snorted at him, but I was impressed. I'd never heard him stand up to her before.

I'd realized then that I hadn't even thought the twins might be doing all this because they wanted their mum and dad to get back together. I'd just assumed they were being **evil for FUN**. I actually started to feel bad for them. It suddenly occurred to me how hard it must be for them with their dad getting married again. Everything would be different for the twins now. Bindi would be moving into their home – into their lives.

That's actually a **LOT** to deal with.

As I'm thinking about last night, Mum comes downstairs, announcing that we're almost ready to go. Another half an hour later we're all waiting outside and Aunty Bindi emerges from the house, beaming with **happiness**. I have to admit, she looks **beautiful**. Her dress is an exact replica of the one that the daughter of some Indian actor wore. (I wasn't really paying attention when she told me.) Anyway, the dress is **HUMONGOUS** and red, with lots of gold lace, jewels and embroidery. It has a **HUGE** puffed-out skirt and she is wearing a jewel-encrusted veil on her head. It's a mixture of Indian and Western fashion, **LOUD** and **PROUD**. It suits her perfectly.

Mustaf is her chauffeur for the day – apparently Uncle Tony is getting to the wedding by special transport, but no one knows what it is! Mustaf holds the door to the limo open proudly as Aunty Bindi shuffles in, **big dress and all**.

Mum squeezes in next to her. Mustaf turns, smiles at me and Milo, and winks.

Milo and he have become firm friends and the kittens are now at Milo's house. His cat Yas took to the kittens instantly and has sort of adopted them. Mustaf is going to visit every day and help Milo find good homes for them – although I have a feeling Mustaf will keep at least one and Milo will definitely try to keep as many as his mum

will allow. You can imagine how **not** happy she
is about that. She has said he can keep the lobster
though, which really surprised me. Milo's grandad
apparently used to keep all kinds of aquatic animals
and has a huge tank which would be perfect for
Larry the lobster. Milo went online and found out
all about keeping Larry safe and making him a home
where he'll be happy and no one will try to cook
him!

Granny says that normally at Indian weddings
the bride's family would travel to the wedding
separately from the groom's family. Obviously,
NOTHING about this wedding has been normal,
so we are all travelling together. A crowd of family
and friends from both sides of the family board the
coach together outside our house and soon we're on
our way.

Granny Jas starts singing old Indian songs,
which sets everyone else off. The twins sit at the
back of the coach. Mindy folds her arms, but then

turns to listen as Manny gets talking to Milo about skateboarding. She even joins in when they start talking about something called a "**360 flip**", which apparently Manny's cousin Indy can do. Mindy says no way, Indy totally made that up!

With all the chattering, it's not long before we pull up at the wedding venue. It's a big old country house hotel, overlooking a huge shimmering lake – nothing but the best for Aunty Bindi.

As the coach parks outside the hotel, I see Aunty Bindi emerging from the limo ahead. Mum ushers her inside to go and freshen up before her **BIG entrance**. Then, as we all get off the coach, Uncle Tony arrives. Not in a normal-looking wedding car or even on a horse...Uncle Tony is sitting high up in a **BIG GOLD TRUCK**! The front of the truck is covered in flowers and lights. There's a huge model of a decorated elephant head on the top of the driver's cabin. It's so beautiful. Along the side of the truck is a big digital sign with photos of

Uncle Tony and Aunty Bindi playing on a loop. It's the craziest thing I've ever seen; it's **HUGE**! Uncle Tony looks like an Indian prince. He is wearing a red turban with coloured strips of sparkling foil hanging from it. It's something Indian grooms have to wear and I always wonder if they can see where they're going. There are drummers playing the dhol and dancers doing a routine in front of the truck as they enter the car park. Behind them I can see all of Uncle Tony's family clapping their hands and singing happily.

For a second, I forget everything and just **marvel** at the **spectacle** moving slowly towards us.

Uncle Tony looks down through the open window at me, smiling a big smile, and says, "Come on, **no dilly-dallying**. Everyone inside. I am getting **MARRIED**, you know! Fancy a lift, you two?" he says to the twins as he opens the truck passenger door. He nods at one of the cousins nearby, who leans down with cupped hands for Manny to step into. Uncle Tony reaches his hand down to Manny, who gladly takes it and grins as he steps into the cousin's hands and climbs up beside his dad.

"How about you, sweetheart?" Uncle Tony asks Mindy.

She huffs and looks away.

"I thought we talked about this last night, Minnie."

I try not to smile. So, it's not just me whose parents call them by a corny nickname. Mindy scowls at her dad even more.

"Look, I don't want you to be unhappy, sweetheart. You children are **so important** to me. I love you. But I love Bindi too. I've never met anyone like her, she makes me so happy and I just think I can be a better dad to you both if I'm **happy**. I'm still always going to be here for you. Nothing will change the fact that I'm your dad and that will always come first. Do you understand?"

Mindy looks around at the crowd of family and friends holding their breath, at the glorious elephant, at the hotel where Aunty Bindi is waiting for her groom, and finally at Uncle Tony's worried face and at Manny, who is shaking his head sadly.

She looks down at the floor and whispers, "Yes. I do want you to be happy, Dad."

There's a **CHEER** from one of the uncles and someone lifts Mindy into the truck, where Uncle Tony hugs her tightly. I think I even see her wipe a tear from her cheek.

"**Come on then, let's get this party started**," Uncle Tony shouts out and the three of them roll forward slowly in the truck.

Everyone follows Uncle Tony, smiling and pointing at the super-sized cheesy photos of the happy couple on the side of the truck.

Milo beams at me. "Anisha Mistry, **you are an actual legend**! You did it! You got everyone to the wedding on time. **You're my hero**," he says proudly. "Orange suits you, by the way. It is the best colour, after all." He rubs his hand over his bright ginger hair and grins. Then he links arms with me and we head into the wedding.

"Oh, by the way, I didn't think you'd mind, I bought a guest with me." He smiles.

"What guest?" I say looking around.

"Ermm, this one!" Milo opens the rather large holdall he's carrying to reveal a plastic box with a shallow pool of treated water, sand, mud and rocks in it and a clicking clacking lobster!

CHAPTER 18

HAPPY EVER AFTERS AND PING-PONG

Once we are all inside, Dad makes sure everyone is seated and Uncle Tony takes his place in the ceremony room. Aunty Bindi, Mum and I stand by the glass doors and wait to make the big entrance. Ages ago Aunty Bindi asked Mum to give her away at the wedding, which I thought was hilarious, until they explained it just means Mum walks down the aisle with her. Bella the dog is carrying the rings, much to Mindy's disgust. Aunty Bindi ordered a special little sparkly doggy outfit for Bella, which she seems to like, if you ask me. I peer through the glass and I can see all of our family and friends sitting waiting inside. My tummy **lurches**. All of a sudden, I'm nervous.

"Aunty, are you **absolutely sure** you want to do this? I mean, look how mean the twins are. They locked their own dad in a coffin and left him there! They really didn't want him to get married. They might be really mean to you. They already put heat rub in your mehndi. Remember how **AWFUL** that was?!"

Aunty Bindi chuckles. "Yes, they are a bit of a handful, aren't they? But I don't know if you've noticed – I've been known to be a bit of a handful myself!" She winks at Mum, who laughs and nods.

"Don't worry, Anni, I can handle them and I think I quite like a bit of **family chaos**. It wouldn't be the same any other way. Besides, I think their bark is worse than their bite. I'll win them round, you'll see. Plus, I have you looking out for me. How lucky am I?" She squeezes my hand.

The three of us look at each other – me, Mum and

my crazy aunt – and I feel a bit **funny** inside. I don't know what it is, but it's a nice kind of **funny**.

The doors open. The room looks **amazing**, I have to admit: the wedding mandap, which is like a gazebo where the ceremony takes place, is made of four gold and crystal pillars and a silk canopy. Under it sits Uncle Tony, along with the priest and an empty throne opposite for Aunty Bindi to sit on. Either side of Uncle Tony are Mindy and Manny. Manny is actually **smiling** and nodding his head to the music, but Mindy **scowls** as one of the aunties tries to put a flower in her hair.

There are pink, white and purple garlands hanging from the ceiling and draped around the pillars of the mandap. The flower delivery man got it right in the end! All our family sit in rows of covered chairs decorated with golden silk bows. They turn to look at us as the music starts. Aunty Bindi's all-time favourite Hindi love song plays: "**Teri Ore**" which means "**Towards You**"I would usually cringe, but I

find myself humming along. **What's that about!?**
As the beat kicks in, Aunty Bindi swishes her dress in time to the music and we walk down the aisle. Uncle Tony nods his head to the song and smiles through the shiny foil strips hanging down from his turban.

I spot Milo waving at me and grinning. Then I notice someone else I know. Hang on, **Beena Bhatt**?

HERE? She's wearing an expensive-looking dress and a fur wrap round her shoulders. She smiles at me sweetly, but it makes my blood run cold.

"Mum, what's she doing here?" I nod in Beena's direction as we walk past.

"Oh, I think that's the daughter of one of Uncle Tony's clients, sweetheart. She seems nice.

Maybe you could invite her round for a playdate? I think she's good friends with the twins," says Mum.

"I'm ten, Mum, not five. Anyway, I have a feeling she'll be busy," I mutter under my breath.

Beena and I are not friends. We're not even close to being friends. Actually, she's my **arch-enemy**. I didn't think I was the type of person to have **arch-enemies**, but then along came Beena Bhatt.

 Beena is the most hideous girl you could meet for the following reasons:

 She has very rich parents and makes sure everyone knows it.

She tells everyone at school that her dad makes super-spy gadgets for the government, but I think he probably just makes something boring like loo roll.

She talks to everyone like they are complete idiots.

Although she herself is very clever, she is also

extremely lazy, which is the reason we became **ARCH-ENEMIES**.

It all started when she cornered Milo and me in the playground one day, and went on and on about letting her use our homework for presentation day in history class, because she was too lazy to do it herself. Anyway, she wouldn't shut up and I just wanted to leave. I was getting all hot and itchy and then **IT** happened. I really didn't mean to knock her down as I pushed past her to make a run for it. But I did and she fell over and everyone in school saw her **PANTS**! It wasn't my fault that it happened. It was an accident!

I push the memory out of my mind. **Now is not the time to be thinking about awful Beena Bhatt!** As we finally get to the front of the room, Aunty Bindi walks up the steps and takes her seat next to Uncle Tony, wearing the biggest smile I've ever seen. Her cheeks are pink and I think she looks like **the happiest person on earth**. I've got my whole family around me and I feel relaxed and calm. Even seeing Beena can't ruin it. This has got to be a first.

The priest says a lot of words in Hindi that I don't really understand, then in Gujarati, English and Punjabi, so everyone gets it. Everybody is smiling and they throw flower petals and rice on the bride and groom and **everyone cheers**. Aunty Bindi looks like she might **explode with joy**. I hear people telling each other how beautiful she looks and how sparkly her dress is and it makes me feel proud that she's my aunty.

There's a bit of a scary moment when the bride and groom are supposed to walk round a holy fire, because the flames keep getting higher and higher. Luckily, Aunty Suki is on hand with the fire extinguisher and a crisis is avoided.

After the ceremony, everyone heads round to

the marquee for the reception, which is basically a fancy word for a big fat party.

In a big function room that then leads out to the marquee there are drinks and snacks, party games and entertainment – there's even table football and ping-pong. The guests mingle and chat happily. Uncle Tony and Aunty Bindi enter to a huge round of applause and lots of hugs from everyone.

"Come and play, Dad!" Manny shouts out from where he and Mindy are standing by the ping-pong table. Uncle Tony looks at Bindi and I see her squeeze his hand as they both walk over.

"Well, you know I was ping-pong champion in my uni days!" Uncle Tony laughs.

"Oh, is that so?" Aunty Bindi says. "Well, so was I!"

They look at each other and at the same time say:

"**PING-PONG BATTLE!**"

"Come on, Manny, you're on my team," Tony tells him.

"Mindy, come and help me!" calls Aunty Bindi.

I look over at Mindy. She's staring at the floor. "No thanks, I'd rather not."

"Come on, do it as a favour to your old dad," says Uncle Tony hopefully. "You might enjoy yourself!"

"I doubt that," mutters Mindy, but she picks up the ping-pong paddle anyway and stands next to Aunty Bindi. Guests gather round to watch as Aunty Bindi turns to Mindy and says, "Let's show them how it's done."

It turns out Aunty Bindi really is a champion ping-pong player and Mindy is pretty good too. When they beat Uncle Tony and Manny (quite quickly!), Mindy is almost smiling.

Bindi puts out her hand to Mindy and says, "Well done, partner. We girls have to stick together. I know I'm not your mum, but maybe we can be friends at least?"

Mindy shrugs, but the scowl has gone – for now, anyway.

Everyone claps and then we move out of the big function toom into the reception inside the marquee. On the black glitter dance floor, under the biggest disco ball I've ever seen, Aunty Bindi and Uncle Tony have their first dance to another old Hindi song. They've been taking lessons, because Bindi said they had to have the best first dance ever. She's been watching a lot of **Strictly Come Dancing**. I'm not sure their instructor was much good though, because Uncle Tony looks like he's holding in a fart and Aunty Bindi is concentrating so hard she's going cross-eyed.

"Poor Tony," Mum chuckles, as she comes over to stand next to me. "You know, Anni, you really saved the day." She slips her arm through mine. For once I don't mind her calling me Anni. I think I might even quite like it.

Dad comes over then and takes Mum's hand and, in a **total cringe moment**, asks her if he can have this dance. Still, it's nice to watch them: Dad with his dad-dancing moves and Mum suddenly all **girly** and **twirly**, which is quite funny.

Then Uncle Ricky takes to the floor in his Elvis suit and everyone claps as he does his special performance. His singing is still **TERRIBLE** but Aunty Bindi and Uncle Tony clearly love the surprise.

Just as I start to feel like everything's pretty much perfect, I see the twins approaching. I look around for an escape route but there isn't one.

"So, Anisha, looks like we are family now, after all." Mindy has a glint in her eye.

"Uh, I guess so," I answer. "I'm sorry I had to

ruin your plan. I couldn't let Aunty Bindi down."

"That's okay." Manny smiles.

Mindy smiles too. "Did you know, Dad is moving us to your school? He said he wants to see more of us...so we'll be seeing a lot more of you."

I realize my mouth is hanging open. The thought of seeing the twins every day is just too horrible.

"Can I ask you something?" I say, feeling brave for a second. "Why did the kidnap note smell of Granny's heat rub? Was that to throw me off the scent, literally?"

"Oh, well, er, no, actually that was accidental. Manny took a spare tube of heat rub from your house the last time we were there just in case we couldn't find any when we needed it for our trick with the mehndi and he put it in his pocket. Do you know how much planning went into this? Anyway, the kidnap note was in that pocket too, and I guess the lid had come off or something." Mindy rolls her eyes at her brother.

"Beena said the note smelled funny but I thought she was being paranoid. But no fear, we will do better next time." She winks, before swishing her hand dramatically and both twins turn to walk away. **UH-OH.**

"Um, no!" I call after them. "I think there's been a misunderstanding. I don't...well that is, I'm not..." I tail off, exhausted.

Mindy looks back and calls over her shoulder. "Don't worry. We'll look after my dad and Bindi on honeymoon. We're going with them, you know!"

"I wouldn't worry," chuckles Milo as he arrives at my side, munching a spicy chicken drumstick. "I just heard your Uncle Tony telling his brother that he's planning on keeping them pretty busy during the honeymoon."

"How?"

"The **kids' club** at the hotel." Milo snorts. "They've got two fun-packed weeks of activities. I hear they have to learn a special song and dance, which they perform for the parents at the end of the holiday!"

I laugh, feeling much better already.

"I'm very proud of you, Anni beta." Granny Jas sneaks up on me again, nearly making me spill my lassi. "You stayed so calm and clever and you saved your auntie's wedding. **WELL DONE**."

"Thanks, Granny," I say. "And thank you for believing in me."

"Ah, now I meant to ask you. Where did that lobster get to? Your daddy does love lobster curry, you know, and as he didn't get it yesterday he was most grumpy!"

I think about Larry the lobster happily clacking away in Milo's makeshift tank just a few metres away. "Oh, I don't know, Granny, he must have escaped. Maybe Dad could try something new? You know he loves your cauliflower curry," I say.

I'm pleased Larry didn't end up as Dad's dinner. I'm going to miss having a lobster around the house but I think he'll be much happier making a home in a proper saltwater aquarium at Milo's house than in a makeshift rock pool under my bed.

Oh no – I've just thought. I hope he didn't wee under there! Anyway Milo spent ages researching how to set up the tank properly and he ran to the pet shop first thing this morning in his best suit to get seawater salt and a bag of sand for Larry. I think they're going to be friends for a long time.

Beena Bhatt waves at me from her table and smiles sweetly. **UH-OH**, what is she up to? Then I see she's on the same table as the twins and they're looking very friendly with each other. And now they're **all** smiling and waving creepily at me.

It's then that the final piece of the puzzle clicks into place. There's only person who could have posted the kidnappers' note through the door: Beena Bhatt! Mindy just said Beena thought the note smelled funny – they must have passed it to her somehow before all this. She must have been helping them all along!

Great, just what I need:

Evil twins

+

Beena Bhatt

=

Triple trouble for me at school!

How many arch-enemies can a girl have?

As the reception goes on, the DJ plays another song and I cringe as I watch Mum and Dad do their "**put the light bulb in**" bhangra moves. All the aunties, uncles, friends and family come onto the dance floor too. Bella the dog is chasing her own tail so fast she looks like a sparkly whirlwind. Milo does his best dance moves and even I do a little side-to-side shuffle at the edge of the dance floor. Milo, looks up smiling.

"Nice moves, Neesh! So, what's next?"

"What do you mean, next? Everything goes back to normal now, maybe even a bit calmer!" I say.

"No way, there must plenty of other mysteries to solve for a daring detective duo like us!"

"I'd rather not if you don't mind. I've had quite enough excitement for one weekend!"

"We'll see." Milo grins confidently. "We make a **BRILLIANT TEAM** and you know it."

I smile too then. He's right of course.

I look back at Aunty Bindi and Uncle Tony. They're doing that embarrassing close-up slow-dancing that grown-ups do and being all smoochy with each other, even though a fast bhangra song is playing now. Aunty Bindi looks up and sees me watching. She waves and winks at me.

I hate to admit it, but maybe my family aren't so bad after all. And maybe, now the wedding's finally happened, I'll get some time to finish my book in peace.

Things can finally be normal, can't they?

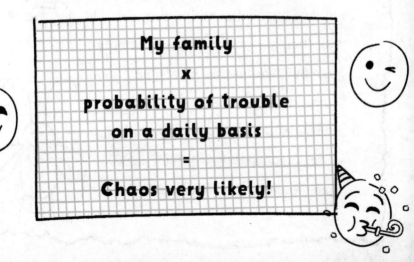

My family
x
probability of trouble
on a daily basis
=
Chaos very likely!

LOBSTER FACT FILE*

Name of animal: Lobster

Scientific name: Nephropidae

Facts:

1. Lobsters have ten legs. Because of this they are called decapods.

2. Lobsters are omnivores, which means they eat anything they can get their claws into. But they mainly like fish, worms and plants, not samosas or pakoras.

3. Lobsters' teeth are actually in their stomachs – and they don't just have one stomach, they have two!

4. Some lobsters can live for up to 100 years (if they don't get caught and cooked!), although a lobster was once recorded as being 140 years old. Imagine that!

5. A lobster can live out of water for up to two days if kept moist and cool.

6. Lobsters wee out of their faces – you have been warned!

* Milo asked me to include this here because, as you know, he is a great lover of animals and he doesn't want you to think the lobster isn't being taken care of. Milo has been putting together an animal fact file for a while now and luckily he has a page on lobsters. If you ever find a lobster on the loose in your house, now you can take good care of it too.

WHO ARE YOU?

**Take this quiz to discover which
ANISHA, ACCIDENTAL DETECTIVE character
you're most like. Will it be Anisha, Aunty Bindi,
Milo or Granny Jas? FIND OUT NOW!**

It's your best friend's birthday. What present do you get them?

a) A rainbow bath bomb for some serious pampering.

b) You bake them a delicious birthday cake.
Home-made treats are the best!

c) You adopt an endangered animal in their name.

d) A specially chosen book about something you know they love.

You've been invited to a fancy-dress party. Do you go as;

a) Your favourite pop star – any excuse to dress up.

b) A zombie – you can't wait to stumble around and spook everyone – tee-hee!

c) An elephant. Animal onesies are so cosy, you practically live in them.

d) An astronaut. It's your dream to wear a real spacesuit one day.

You have to do a school project on someone you're interested in. You choose:

a) Coco Chanel, one of the world's most famous and glamorous fashion designers.

b) Sophia Duleep Singh, rebellious Indian suffragette and god-daughter of Queen Victoria.

c) David Attenborough. His TV shows about animals and our planet are amazing.

d) Marie Curie. Her research into radioactivity used science to help people – and she won a Nobel prize.

If you were an animal, you would be...

a) A unicorn. Okay, so they're not technically real, but they are super cool and sparkly – like you!

b) A raccoon. They might look sweet but they're really cheeky and will do anything for a snack.

c) A dog. Loyal, energetic, playful and a best friend people can always rely on.

d) A kitten. Playful, curious and clever, and always accidentally getting up to mischief.

Okay, so do you remember your answers? Turn the page to find out which ANISHA, ACCIDENTAL DETECTIVE character YOU are.

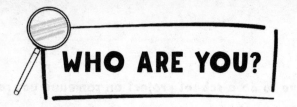

WHO ARE YOU?

MOSTLY As.
You're Aunty Bindi!

Stylish and glamorous, you love a little bit of luxury. You're fun to be around, have a heart of gold, and can't help but bring a little bit of sparkle and star quality with you wherever you go.

MOSTLY Bs.
You're Granny Jas!

You may look like the quiet type, but inside you're mega feisty and fiery. Bursting with energy, you're the life and soul of the party...with a good dollop of mischief too.

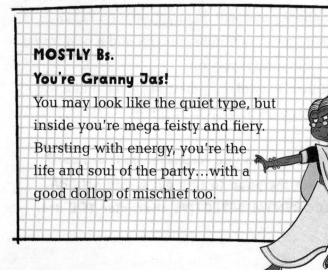

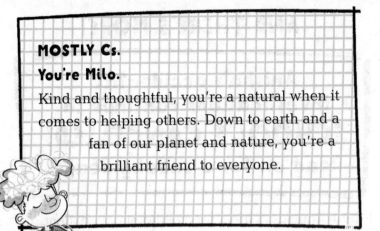

MOSTLY Cs.
You're Milo.
Kind and thoughtful, you're a natural when it comes to helping others. Down to earth and a fan of our planet and nature, you're a brilliant friend to everyone.

MOSTLY Ds.
You're Anisha
Wow, you're one smart cookie! Clever and curious, you love nothing more than curling up with a good book. However, as much as you prefer a quiet life, you're so engaged with the world that adventure always finds you.

You might be a mix of characters, because there's something for everyone in **ANISHA, ACCIDENTAL DETECTIVE.**

AND THERE'S MORE!

Anisha's accidental investigations continue in
SCHOOL'S CANCELLED!
Read on for a sneaky peak...

I think Thursdays are a funny kind of day. It's not the weekend yet, which is okay with me because weekends mean family time. Family time usually means a lot of noise and drama in our house. Don't get me wrong, I do love my family, but they're also a bit bonkers and they get themselves into trouble **A LOT**. Anyway, this Thursday is kind of a special and exciting day at school because of the **BIG ANNOUNCEMENT**!

You see, there's a science fair next week. And not just any science fair either. It's the National Schools Science Fair and whoever has the best experiment wins an amazing prize. Actually, not just amazing, it's an *intergalactic* prize – a trip to an international space centre! And the winner gets to meet a real-life astronaut! How cool is that?

Everyone in my year is so excited, even the kids who don't normally like science. Each school can only enter two teams and today our science teacher, Miss Bunsen, is going to announce who our two teams are. She's been watching us working on our projects for the last four weeks and it's been making my tummy go all weird, because I want our team to be one of the chosen ones **SO BAD**!

Mostly I quite like school, apart from some of the other kids. When I say other kids, I actually mean the evil twins Mindy and Manny, my cousins (only by marriage – their dad, Uncle Tony, married my mum's sister, Aunty Bindi). And yes, I meant it when I said they're **EVIL**. They used to go to a boarding school, but Uncle Tony decided it would be better for them to be close to home, where he can keep an eye on them. It's weird, but since they've been at my school they seem to be staying out of trouble. I keep an eye on them though, as they are not to be trusted.

If that wasn't enough to deal with, I also have an arch-enemy, Beena Bhatt – she's the worst. She thinks *I'm* her arch-enemy but I'm really not. I might have **ACCIDENTALLY** knocked her over once but that doesn't mean we have to forever be arch-enemies! I have tried to tell her that but she won't listen, so now I just try to stay out of her way. It's not easy. I'd ask to be homeschooled, but that would probably be worse!

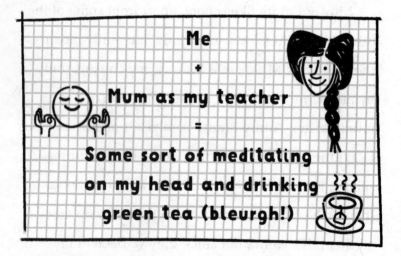

Me
+
Mum as my teacher
=
Some sort of meditating
on my head and drinking
green tea (bleurgh!)

On the other hand…

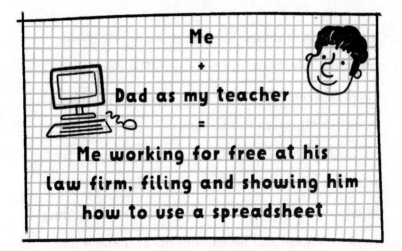

Me

+

Dad as my teacher

=

Me working for free at his law firm, filing and showing him how to use a spreadsheet

But then what about...

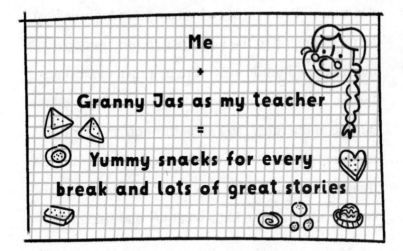

Me

+

Granny Jas as my teacher

=

Yummy snacks for every break and lots of great stories

I smile to myself, thinking about how fun it would be to read my books all day while Granny cooked up a mountain of treats. She's making paratha* this morning, which are my favourite. The delicious smell of a big pile of steaming fried spicy flatbreads is wafting through the house.

Dad already left at 8.14 a.m., which is exactly fourteen minutes later than he should have done. He blustered out of the door in a whirlwind of jangling keys, briefcase and files under his arm and a half-eaten piece of toast dangling between his teeth. I don't think I've ever seen him sit down for breakfast. Mum's gone off to the local gym to run her early morning meditation class. I'm in a rush too, because I woke up late. I was up reading by torchlight till the middle of the night, so I slept through my alarm this morning. It was Dad's morning bathroom noises that finally woke me. I once saw a documentary about camels and weirdly that's what my dad sounds like

---

* Parathas are just the best. They are spicy chapatis and no one makes them like Granny Jas.

– gargling and gurgling every morning. For once I was glad that he's so loud!

I grab a paratha from the plate Granny's piling them onto and stuff it in my mouth too fast. "Hot, hot, hot!" I gasp, as Granny passes me a glass of water without even turning around.

"You kids, always in a rush. Take your time, silly," she gently scolds.

"But I am in a rush, I'm gonna be late," I moan.

"You shouldn't stay up till who knows what time then!" Granny smiles. "You think I don't see your torch light shining under the bedroom door as I go to my room at night? When will you learn, Granny sees everything!"

"In my defence, I was reading a maths book!" I protest. "We have a test on Thursdays. It's my favourite subject! Well, it used to be."

"Used to be?" Granny studies my face. "Has something happened, beta?"

"No...I mean...well, it's just I usually know the

answer when the teacher asks a question and…"

"And that's a bad thing these days, is it? Don't be shy, beta. You should never be afraid to show your talents. You are clever. If the teacher asks you a question, go ahead and answer."

"You don't understand," I sigh.

Granny waves her rolling pin in my direction. "Granny understands everything."

"I just think sometimes it's easier to try and blend in, be part of the crowd. Not everyone in my school thinks being clever is cool."

"Humph," Granny snorts. "Anni, what are you talking about? Why would you want to hide your light? You must stand out, stand up, be proud!" She puffs out her chest.

"Do you think we would be here if our ancestors had just sat there idly letting everyone else speak up for them? No, of course not!"

I don't really know why Granny talks about people who lived long ago when things are so different now. I couldn't be any less like my brave ancestors if I tried – speaking up isn't really my thing.

"It's not that easy these days, Granny. If you're too clever, then some of the other kids make fun of you for being a nerd. I never used to care in Year Four or even Year Five, but things seem different in Year Six. There are still lots of kids who want to study and do well, but the teacher always uses my work as an example and it's embarrassing. It's just not good to be too clever."

"Too clever? Too clever? What is that? You can never be too clever, beta. Your brain is your super power, it's the thing that makes you special. Only you think like you!"

"Well, I wish someone would tell certain kids in my school that being clever is super."

"I will tell them! Shall I come to school with you now? I will put on my chappals* and march down to that school and I will tell them!"

"No, no, it's fine, Granny – anyway, grown-ups aren't allowed into school and I'd, erm, better go!" I make a move towards the front door before Granny can put her chappals or anything else on and follow me.

She shouts after me, "Put your hood up, it's cold out there! That nice weatherman, Gopal Singh – you know, the handsome one? – he said we might get some rain later…"

WILL ANISHA AND MILO TRIUMPH AT THE NATIONAL SCHOOLS SCIENCE FAIR? OR WILL THEY FACE AN EXPLOSIVE DISASTER?

FIND OUT IN ANISHA'S NEXT ADVENTURE...

OUT NOW!

LOOK OUT FOR ANISHA'S THIRD CASE...

COMING SOON!

Milo and I have been looking forward to this half-term for what feels like FOREVER – we're finally going to the National Space Centre, to meet a real-life space engineer!

My whole family wanted to tag along and visit a festival first, where this super-famous, mega-expensive diamond is on display. But guess what? The diamond has been STOLEN! And the police think MY GRANNY did it so she's in serious TROUBLE.

Someone needs to prove Granny Jas is innocent, so it looks like Milo and I might need to go UNDERCOVER.

It's lucky I'm Anisha, Accidental Detective!

ACKNOWLEDGEMENTS

Well, this feels weird to even be writing acknowledgements but I have to say a few special thanks to those who got me here. Because my writing is only one part of the story and so many others have made it a real thing.

Firstly, to my agent, the wonderful Kate Shaw. Thank you for guiding me when necessary (quite often!) and for listening to my worries (even more often!) and for cheering me on every step of the way.

To everyone at Usborne, my everlasting thanks for believing in me and for investing all your knowledge and expertise in my stories. Special gratitude to Stephanie King, my most excellent editor and the awesome force that is Rebecca Hill for her wisdom and for taking a chance on me. Katarina Jovanovic and Fritha Lindqvist, your PR expertise are second to none. Thank you for everything.

To the astoundingly talented Emma McCann, your illustrations have brought my story to life, thank you so much for being part of this bonkers series.

How can I ever thank the extraordinary Emma Greenwood enough for believing in my writing and for finding the right words in my pages of waffle!

So much love too for my fellow Foundies. All we had when we started were a few story ideas and far too much colourful stationery. And to Imogen at GEA, my heartfelt thanks for nudging me gently but firmly in front of the right people.

My gratitude continues with the awe-inspiring community of SCWBI and the Undiscovered Voices team. You changed the course of my life when you chose my story and thank you just isn't big enough.

My fellow Usbornites, AM Howell, Samuel J Halpin and